My Name is Konisola

MY NAME IS
KONISOLA

Alisa Siegel

Second Story Press

Library and Archives Canada Cataloguing in Publication

Title: My name is Konisola / Alisa Siegel.
Names: Siegel, Alisa, author.
Identifiers: Canadiana (print) 20190187034 | Canadiana (ebook) 20190187069 | ISBN 9781772601190 (softcover) | ISBN 9781772601206 (EPUB)
Classification: LCC PS8637.I27 M9 2020 | DDC jC813/.6—dc23

Editors: Heather Camlot and Kathryn Cole

Cover illustration © Talya Baldwin, i2iart.com

Printed and bound in Canada

Second Story Press gratefully acknowledges the support of the Ontario Arts Council and the Canada Council for the Arts for our publishing program. We acknowledge the financial support of the Government of Canada through the Canada Book Fund.

Published by
SECOND STORY PRESS
20 Maud Street, Suite 401
Toronto, ON M5V 2M5
www.secondstorypress.ca

For Noam and Daniel

This is a story of generosity. Of how open-hearted strangers stepped into the life of a mother and a child. Of how remarkable coincidences, good fortune, and human connections rescued a young girl. And of how darkness became light.

ONE

The memory box is made of a dark wood.
It's rectangular, about the size of a shoebox.
Inside, some gold hoop earrings.
A few bracelets. A thick necklace.
A worn pink leather wallet.
A slim red diary.
A photo of a woman and a young girl.
These are her most precious possessions.

Konisola presses her nose tightly against the airplane window. She can make out the streets and houses of the city below. Is that her school, over there? Or is that it, farther to the left? When she twists her neck, she can see cars and trucks inching slowly forward. Gradually, everything on the ground becomes smaller and smaller. She strains her eyes, trying to keep the objects sharp. But it's no use. Everything turns to dots.

Konisola has never been on an airplane before. She's only seen them in books at school and overhead in the sky. She always dreamed of being able to fly.

She just never imagined it would happen so soon. Or in this way.

Just a few hours earlier, she and her friends were outside at recess. "You're IT, Konisola!" they yelled. It was her turn to be the chaser. They were playing *Boju-Boju*, their version of hide and seek.

"Watch out! I'm coming to get you!" Konisola laughed and screamed as she sped around the yard. She was nine years old, younger than some of her friends, older than others, taller and faster than all of them. She tagged one after the other. Her chest felt like it would explode. Just as she was about to catch the last one, she stopped abruptly.

There was her mother at the edge of the schoolyard, two knapsacks at her feet. What was she doing here in the middle of the day?

Her mother motioned to Konisola from the fence. Konisola's heart pounded as she ran to greet her.

"Mama!"

Six days had passed since she saw her last. *Six days since that terrible night.* Konisola's mind raced with a thousand questions. She saw her mother pull at the folds of skin between her thumb and pointer finger. She always did this when she was nervous. And her mother was wearing large, dark sunglasses. Not large enough to hide the dark shadow on her cheekbone, still bruised and swollen.

"Come quickly," her mother whispered in her ear. She took her firmly by the hand. "We must go."

"Go? But it's the middle of the day. Where do we have to go?"

"I'll explain later. Hurry now!" her mother said sharply. "We don't have time." She yanked Konisola toward the street.

What is happening? Konisola wondered. *Why is she taking me out of school and away from my friends? Why now?*

"I don't want to go yet!" she shouted, louder than she had intended. She dug in her heels and pulled in the opposite direction. "We're in the middle of a game and Teacher has a special art project planned for us this afternoon."

"Konisola, this is more important! We have to get out, before they see us. Quickly now! Don't be difficult," her mother hissed. "We must not call attention to ourselves. If we do, all will be lost."

Konisola shuddered. Who were *they?* And *what* would be lost? She had no idea. But she saw the steel in mother's eyes and knew she had to go. She looked back at her friends playing in the schoolyard. It would be the last time she would see them.

❄ ❄ ❄

A black car stood waiting on the roadside. Konisola and her mother slipped inside. It was steaming hot, hotter even than outside. Konisola's legs felt wet and sticky on the vinyl seat. She played with the buttons on the door and lowered the car window.

"Close it, Konisola!" her mother snapped.

"But I'm boiling. I need air."

"Close it quickly! We cannot be seen by anyone."

"Why not? Where are we going?"

Her mother fumbled with some papers. Her hands were shaking. On one document, Konisola saw a photo of herself with some writing.

"We are going away. Far away."

Away? She and her mother never went away.

"You must be brave, Konisola," her mother said. "We must do this so that you will be safe."

❋ ❋ ❋

The airplane climbs into the sky. Konisola's questions multiply and she can't hold them in.

"Where are we going?" she asks her mother again.

"To another country. To Canada. No one will hurt us anymore."

"Where is Canada?" she presses. "Where will we live?"

"We will see, *Oyinkan*, my honey. No more questions now."

Konisola cups her hands over her ears. The sound of wind whistles in her head.

"My ears feel funny," she announces loudly, "like something is stuffed inside of them."

"Try swallowing, child," a woman behind them suggests through the space between the seats. "If your mother allows it, I can give you some chewing gum. That helps too."

Her mother's eyes are already closed, her breathing heavy with sleep.

"My mother says I can have some gum, please," Konisola says softly to the woman behind.

The woman reaches her hand between the seats and gives her a stick of gum. Konisola unwraps it quietly and begins to chew. Her mouth fills with sweet water. She rests her head against the back of her seat. She chews and swallows, chews and swallows. Her ears clear.

"Canada." She repeats the word to herself. *"Canada."*

TWO

The airport in Toronto is big and busy. Konisola and her mother follow the crowd of travelers. Down escalators. Along wide hallways. Past restaurants and shops. Until they reach a large room with officers in bulky uniforms, guns tucked into their holsters.

"Citizens to the right. Visitors to the left," someone hollers. "Have your passports ready!"

The two of them drift forward in the thick forest of people. Konisola takes her mother's hand. It's cold and damp. It feels like fear. But there's also the comforting jangle of her mother's bracelets. Konisola knows how much her mother loves the few pieces of jewelry she owns. Today she wears it all: along with the bangles… the necklace, the blue earrings.

They stand in a line that snakes around the room. Konisola's legs ache. She releases herself from her mother's grip, wiggles her toes, and twists her feet. As she does, her sandals touch the red tape on the ground.

"Don't step over the line until the officer calls us!" her mother warns. "Keep very quiet. If they ask you a question, pretend you do not understand. Do not say anything." She takes back Konisola's hand, squeezes it tightly.

Konisola watches her mother's eyes dart anxiously from one side of the room to the other. Beads of sweat drip down her forehead. Her mother has done everything needed to get them here, to Canada. But now she's hunched over, her spirit crushed. She raises her hands to her face and begins to weep quietly.

"It's okay, Mama. Don't cry. I'll help you." Konisola strokes her mother's arm.

"What is the matter? Why are you crying?" It's the woman from the plane, the one with the chewing gum. She's Nigerian too.

"We have nowhere to go," Konisola's mother says. "We have nothing. No one. We had to run away." She tells the stranger bits and pieces of their story. Their lives were in danger. They had to flee. Someone helped to get them documents and tickets to Canada, but now they are completely alone. "My name is Abimbola," she whispers.

The stranger listens, and then she leans in and speaks softly. "My name is Ayodele. Friends call me Ayo. You can stay with me—but just for a few days." She quickly jots something down on a piece of paper. "Here. This is my address. You'll need it to give to the officers so they can keep track of you. Tell them I am a friend. Nothing else. If they allow you to enter, I will meet you on the other side."

Konisola stares at the woman. *Who is this stranger, and why is she helping us in this way?*

"Next!" the officer calls.

It's their turn.

Konisola looks up at the man and shudders. His face is chiseled and serious.

"Name?" the officer demands, his voice cold and stern.

"I am Abimbola. This is my daughter, Konisola." Her mother's voice, usually strong and confident, is shaky.

"How old are you, Konisola?"

"Nine."

"Who is this beside you?"

"My mother."

The officer turns his attention back to Abimbola. "Where's her father?"

"Dead."

There's a pause. "Purpose of your trip?" he asks. "Why are you here?"

"We need protection," her mother says haltingly. "We cannot go home. If we are sent back, terrible things will happen to us."

Konisola has never heard her mother talk

like this, or look like this, even when she was beaten by Uncle.

Even then, her mother never seemed to lose her gumption, her pride. Now her lips are pinched tightly together. Her body is trembling. Her long face, once so full and strong, looks narrow and gaunt. This new, unfamiliar version of her mother scares Konisola.

The officer eyes them. He marks some papers with a red pen. *What does that mean? Have we done something wrong? Could we be sent to prison? Or sent back home?*

The officer calls for another immigration official who leads them to a closed room marked Canada Border Services Agency. A security guard watches as the officer searches their small bags.

"Where are you from?" he demands.

"Lagos, Nigeria."

"Who do you know here?"

"We are alone," her mother answers nervously, and then catches herself. "We have only one friend," she stumbles on the words. "We will stay with her. This is her address." She shows him the slip of paper. He eyes it—and them—suspiciously.

"Why did you come?"

"Our lives were in danger."

Konisola's heart drums. Her mother shifts uncomfortably and pulls again at the skin on her hand. The officer leaves the room with the papers. They wait and wait. When the officer returns, he hands them a list of instructions. Forms to fill out. Dates. Rules. And then he stamps a page.

"Make sure to let Immigration know if your address changes. You'll receive a letter in the mail, a Notice to Appear before the Refugee Protection Division," he says. "The notice will include the date, time, and address of your hearing. A decision will be made then. Either you'll be allowed to stay, or you'll be sent back to your country of origin." He pauses and looks at them once more. His face softens a little.

"Welcome to Canada," he says.

They're free to go. For now.

THREE

The cold is shocking.

Konisola's body buckles as she steps out of the airport and into the biting February air. The wind howls, the ground crunches beneath her feet. She's never felt anything like it. Her thin clothes and sandals, perfect for the warm weather back home, are all wrong for a frigid Canadian winter night.

Her toes feel numb. The bitterness rises through her legs and the rest of her body. Her breath shivers. Her teeth chatter. She bends down to touch the strange white powder, studies the thin, delicate crystals that melt on her hand.

Her first snow.

They follow the stranger, Ayo, as if in a dream. *Who is she?* Konisola wonders again. Her mother has to trust the stranger. There's little choice.

They board a large bus. Konisola looks out the foggy window. With her index finger, she traces her name on the glass. Through the markings, she can make out bits and pieces of the snow-covered highway. Her eyes feel as heavy as stone. She fights to keep them open but soon falls into a deep sleep.

❄ ❄ ❄

"Konisola," her mother says, shaking her. "Konisola, we must get off. This is our stop."

It's late at night as they trail behind Ayo. The fierce wind slaps Konisola's face and body and howls in her ears. The snow lands on her eyelashes. It's hard to see.

A desert of snow, she thinks.

They press on. No one speaks. Konisola opens her mouth to catch snowflakes on her tongue. As the wind whips her face, she wonders if she'll turn to ice too.

How much farther? Where are we going?

FOUR

When she opens her eyes, sunlight is pouring in from a window.

Konisola is under a gray blanket on a sofa, her legs are tangled with those of her mother, who lies curled up on the opposite end.

Konisola surveys the room. The walls are lime green. There isn't much furniture. A small white table with four black chairs. A poster of a tree. A television.

Her mother stirs.

"We made it, Konisola," she says in a half-sleep. "We are here."

"Where is *here?*" Konisola demands. "Why

did we come here?" All the confusion, fear, and anger swells inside her. "Why did you bring me to this strange place? I want to go home!"

"We are *not* going home, Konisola. We will start new lives here. Home is not safe for us. Don't you remember what happened?" Her mother's sharp voice slices through her.

Of course, she remembers.

Her father died in a car accident. After that, everything changed. She and her mother had to go live with her father's brother, Konisola's uncle. They had no choice—that was the tradition. Her mother was a free spirit, a quality her husband had admired. But Uncle wouldn't tolerate it.

"You must know your place," he threatened. "This is *my* house. You are living under *my* roof. *You* will obey *me!*"

"No one will tell me what to do. Not you or anyone!" her mother spat back. She wanted Konisola to be strong and proud too.

"You must be like the greatest women of

Nigeria," her mother told her late at night in the quiet of their shared room. She whispered their names into Konisola's ear so Uncle wouldn't hear. "Like Oyinkansola Abayomi, whose name you share. Like Abiola and Pelewura." They had fought for the rights of Nigerian women. "And like Moremi Ajasoro, Queen of Ile-Ife." Her mother spoke of her often. Queen Moremi was celebrated for her great courage and for bringing peace, prosperity, and progress to her people.

Her mother and Uncle argued a lot. He had a terrible temper, became enraged quickly. Abimbola wouldn't back down. Konisola remembered the last fight. The yelling, the screaming, the brutality. She and her mother were in the kitchen when Uncle stormed in. Anger burned in his eyes and in his voice.

"How dare you defy me! You will do as I say!" he thundered. He pointed his long, thick finger at Abimbola's face. "You *and* your daughter will show me respect!"

Konisola hated Uncle. Hated him for the terrible things he said of her mother and all that he did. But that night was different from all the others. Uncle's rage was wilder than usual. Konisola watched in horror as he grabbed her mother's arm, slapped her hard across the face with his ringed fingers. She saw his clenched fists. Her mother fought back, but he was much stronger.

"Go to your room and lock the door, Konisola!" her mother shouted. "Do not let anyone in!"

Konisola didn't want to leave her mother's side. She wanted to stay and protect her.

"Go! *Now!*" her mother yelled, louder, harder this time. Konisola ran. From inside her room, she peeked through the crack in the door and watched. When she couldn't look anymore, she hid under the bed and plugged her ears. But it wasn't enough. The screams punctured the walls. She heard a swift, loud crash followed by a terrifying silence. And then the shrill sound of sirens.

"Your mother got what she deserved!" Uncle yelled after her from the other side of the door. "Be careful, or you will too."

Konisola didn't come out from under the bed that night. She stayed in her room the following day. There was no sign of her mother the next day or the following. With each passing day, she became more afraid. She didn't see her mother again until that morning in the schoolyard. Six days later.

Now, here in Ayo's apartment, Konisola avoids her mother's gaze.

"We must do this, Oyinkan." *Oyinkan. Honey.* The nickname that her mother uses when she speaks gently to her. "We must do this so that you will be safe," her mother repeats.

Nothing about this feels safe to Konisola.

FIVE

They walk side by side on the snow and slush-covered streets of Ayo's neighborhood. Konisola likes seeing her reflection beside her mother's in the shop windows. *My beautiful mother, so graceful and so tall.* Konisola is tall too. Her complexion is dark. She wears her hair in many long tight braids—cornrows.

To keep warm, Konisola wears winter clothes borrowed from Ayo. The thick sweater feels strange. It scratches her skin. She's never felt anything like it before. Everything is so bulky. Her feet slide around inside the boots.

Just minutes after they set out, her mother

stops suddenly, draws in a short, sharp breath. "Come, Konisola. We must go back," her mother says. "I need to rest." Her mother moves slowly. When they reach the apartment, she stretches out on the sofa that is their shared bed and closes her eyes.

Rest. Sleep. That's all her mother seems to want to do now. Each walk is shorter than the last. *Why is she so tired all the time?* Konisola wonders.

For three days straight they stay in the apartment. There isn't much for Konisola to do. She pokes around, cleans the dishes, and colors. Her mother hardly moves from the couch. She sleeps a great deal. When she's awake, she sifts through bits of paper. Each has a name and telephone number. Some she received at the airport, a few from Ayo.

She writes them all down in a slim red-and-black book. Her diary. She never lets it out of her sight.

She has another book that's always with her

too. The Qur'an, a Muslim prayer book. On the outside, it's a light and wrinkled gray, like an elephant's dry skin. Inside, the pages are a hot pink. Konisola's favorite color.

The fourth day begins like the previous three, but it will end very differently.

Konisola wakes up feeling grumpy and restless. She feels like she'll jump out of her skin if she's stuck inside the apartment for one more day.

Her mother sighs. "All right, my girl. Let's go out for a little while."

The two walk to a nearby pharmacy. "Go look around," her mother says. "I have to speak to the pharmacist."

Konisola wanders up and down the aisles.

Toothpaste.

Greeting cards.

Shampoo.

Cookies.

Chocolate.

How I'd love some of that chocolate. Her mouth waters looking at the treats. She wants to taste them, but she knows there's no money to spare. She sees how carefully her mother counts each bill, each coin that she keeps in the old and tattered pink wallet she brought from home. What little she has, she gives to Ayo for food.

Her mother appears beside her. "Let's go," she says softly.

They make their way toward the exit. But before they reach the door, Konisola feels her mother grab her shoulder, dig her fingers into her sweater. A moment later, her mother collapses and falls to the floor.

"Mama!" Konisola gasps. "Mama! What's wrong? Wake up!" No answer. Her mother lies still. Her eyes are closed. Panic rises in Konisola's throat. Noise roars in her ears. "*Help!*" she shrieks. "Please, someone help!" Everything swirls around Konisola. Strangers begin to run and shout. In minutes, red lights flash through the storefront windows.

Two medics hoist Abimbola onto a stretcher and rush her into the waiting ambulance. Konisola climbs in beside her. Her mother lies flat, an oxygen mask on her face, eyes opening and closing. Konisola strokes her mother's hand, in that special spot between her thumb and her pointer finger. The sirens scream as the ambulance races through unfamiliar streets.

SIX

Konisola squints against the sharp white lights of the hospital emergency room. So many sick people. Some hobble on crutches, others lie on stretchers, many are slumped in chairs.

Abimbola is taken to a small curtained room.

A tall man in matching green pants and top, a stethoscope wrapped around his neck, asks Konisola some questions. She doesn't know what her mother would want her to say. She tells him all she knows—that her mother is tired and weak all the time.

And then she's told to wait outside. She

stands on the other side of the curtain, leans in, and listens. The doctor speaks softly to her mother. Konisola strains to hear the muffled voices.

"Tests."

"How long?"

"Daughter."

As soon as the doctor leaves the room, Konisola, heart hammering against her chest, rushes to her mother's bedside. "Mama!" She lays her head on her mother's chest.

"Listen carefully, Konisola." Abimbola's voice is weak. "I must stay in the hospital. I need some tests."

"I'll stay with you," Konisola says quickly.

"No. You cannot. You will stay with Ayo. She will come for you later tonight, after work."

"*No!* I don't want to go. I want to stay with *you.*" Konisola feels scared. She tries not to cry. How can they be apart now, in this strange place where they know no one?

"You must go Konisola."

SEVEN

And now here she is, in a different small apartment, far from the hospital and from her mother. Far, even, from Ayo.

Konisola stayed with her for a few days. But then Ayo was called out of town, to care for her own sick mother back home in Nigeria.

"I have a friend," Ayo told her. "You can stay with her until I get back."

This woman, like Ayo, has to work at a job all day and into the evening. But in every other way, they're different.

"Ayodele needed a favor, so I agreed to let you stay," the woman said. "But that's it. Nothing more. I'm busy. I can't take you places. I can't cook and clean for you. You'll have to do your part."

Konisola isn't allowed to go out by herself. She spends long, lonely hours in the apartment with a list of don'ts:

Don't make noise.

Don't make a mess.

Don't open the door.

Don't go outside.

Don't let anyone in.

"Be good," the woman warns before she leaves in the morning. "The walls have eyes."

Konisola imagines the eyes. Eyeballs on the walls and on the ceiling. Eyeballs on the table and in the food. Eyeballs in the slices of bread and bobbing in the water.

How did this happen? How did I end up here, alone? She can't go out to play and she isn't sent to school. Instead, she spends her days doing chores. She washes dishes, folds laundry, and sweeps the floors, the way her mother taught her back home.

In the middle of the night, Konisola wakes feeling scared and confused. She flails her arms, struggles to see in the dark. Tries to remember where she is. She pictures her mother's face, her big dark eyes, her long neck. Tries to conjure her deep voice. Her loud bursts of laughter. She hasn't heard that laughter in a long time.

During the day, Konisola stares at the phone. She wishes it would ring. She tries to *make* it ring. She picks it up and listens for the dial tone, just to be sure it's working.

It is.

She's spoken to her mother only twice since leaving her in the hospital.

"Come and get me!" She wants to yell both times she hears her mother's voice. But she doesn't yell. She doesn't cry. She doesn't complain.

"When are you coming for me?" she asks.

"Soon, Konisola."

"*When* is soon? I want to be with you. I can look after you," she pleads. The words catch in her throat. "*Please*, Mama."

"I wish I could. But it is not possible yet. Listen carefully, Konisola! If you are ever in trouble and need help, call Nurse Colleen. She is one of my nurses at the hospital, and a friend. Here is her number. Keep it with you. No matter what."

Konisola writes the number on a small piece of paper. She rehearses it until she knows it by heart. She keeps the paper tucked into her pocket. Many times a day, she feels for it to make sure it's there. At night, she places it under her pillow. Before she sleeps, she whispers the number once more into the stillness of the room. And early in the morning, when she wakes, it's the first thing she reaches for.

The days drag on and on.

How many weeks have they been apart? Three? Four? She's lost track. Each day feels like forever as she waits for her mother to come and get her.

With no one to talk to and nothing to do, Konisola is bored and anxious. She knows she doesn't belong inside these walls. She wants to go outside, to be with kids her own age.

From the balcony, she watches enviously as the neighborhood children race to the nearby school, knapsacks flip-flopping on their backs. At 8:55 a.m. on the nose, the bell rings. She listens for it again to signal lunch at 11:55 a.m., and then again at 3:30 in the afternoon to mark the end of the school day. It's her favorite sound. The only sound that pierces the silence of her day.

I should be with them, she thinks. *I should be in school too!*

One afternoon, while she cleans inside a cupboard, Konisola discovers a thick pad of blank pages. How she loves to draw. "You have talent, Konisola. Keep drawing," her teacher back home used to say.

Konisola sits down at the kitchen table with a pencil and begins. Slowly at first, and then looser, faster, her hand dances on the page. She sketches a picture of herself and her mother in a park. It feels good to be drawing again. As soon as she finishes, she hides the paper under her mattress, along with several blank pages. She'll draw a new picture each day, she promises herself, until she and her mother are together.

And then she has an idea.

She takes a fresh piece of paper and folds the edges this way and that. "HELLO!" she writes inside. "I'M HERE. LOOK UP!" Konisola goes out to the balcony, stretches her arm back as far as it can go and sends her paper plane out into the world. It glides up and forward and then begins to sink, twirling and fluttering down to the ground below.

Feeling bolder, Konisola waits for the familiar clinking of keys in the lock. When the woman walks through the door, Konisola braces herself and utters the few short words she's rehearsed all day long.

"I want to go to school."

"Go to school?" the woman snaps. "I can't send you to school! You don't live here. We could get into trouble, with Immigration, with the police. Who knows what might happen if they ask too many questions? No. It's not possible."

Konisola remembers the Immigration Officer's words at the airport. There would be a refugee hearing to decide if they would be allowed to stay. A notice would come in the mail—with the date. *When will that happen? And how will they find us now that we are no longer at Ayo's?*

That night, lying in bed, staring at the ceiling, Konisola's mind spins with one terrifying possibility. *What if my mother isn't coming back?*

EIGHT

The next afternoon, Konisola reaches into her pocket and pulls out the worn piece of paper with Nurse Colleen's phone number on it. She stares at it, just as she has a hundred times before.

In the distance, she hears the school bell ringing. She thinks back to her last day in school, and to the night she and her mother arrived. The snow-covered ground. The howling winds. It's sunny outside now. The season has changed. The children are wearing sweaters and light jackets. Buds are bursting on the trees. But to Konisola it feels all wrong.

I don't belong here, in this apartment. I am not supposed to be here.

"Call if you are in trouble," her mother had said.

Should I call? Or wait just a little longer?

Maybe tomorrow her mother will finally come for her.

The pang in Konisola's chest tells her otherwise.

She draws in a great, deep breath, and begins to dial.

NINE

It's Friday afternoon when Nurse Colleen's cell phone rings. On the other end, Konisola swallows hard. Stands up as straight as she can.

"I want to see my mother," she says. "Please. I need to see her."

"Konisola?" Nurse Colleen can hardly believe it. "Is that you?"

Nurse Colleen knew all about Konisola. She'd known about her for weeks.

Soon after Abimbola was first admitted to the hospital, Colleen began to hear rumblings and murmurs about a complicated patient from the other nurses.

"That woman doesn't trust anyone," someone said. "She's afraid of needles," said another. "And she's difficult."

"Difficult" didn't scare Nurse Colleen. And "that woman" sounded like she needed a friend. Someone to talk to. Nurse Colleen began to visit Abimbola often. Abimbola began to trust this nurse, to open up to her.

Abimbola had been through many medical tests and procedures. And the results were bad. Advanced colon cancer. It turned out that she had been sick for some time but had told no one.

"I *had* to keep it a secret," she confessed to Colleen one day. "My brother-in-law believes in bad omens, in the power of the evil eye. If he'd known I was sick, life would have been even worse."

"But why did you choose to come to Canada?" Colleen asked. "Wasn't there somewhere else, somewhere closer?"

"Somewhere else? *Tsk.*" Abimbola clicked her tongue. "Where is somewhere? I had nowhere to go, *no one* to turn to. And I was afraid. If we stayed in our country, even in another city, Uncle would have found us—forced us to return. I had to get away, as far as possible. I met a woman. 'Go to Canada,' she said. 'You and your child will be taken care of. Go, while you still can.' I gave her some money. She helped us get out."

Colleen listened. She worried about Abimbola, sick and alone in a new country. Together, she and Abimbola notified the Immigration and Refugee authorities that Abimbola was in hospital. Colleen began to spend more and more time with Abimbola, to have lunch at her bedside. She stayed with her during medical check-ups and tests. She visited on weekends too, when the hospital was quiet and lonely. She brought slippers, a robe, and the spicy foods Abimbola craved.

Colleen showed Abimbola photos of her two children—her son who loved baseball, her daughter who danced.

"My daughter likes to dance too," Abimbola said. "To dance and to draw." She told Colleen about good times in her life back home. About growing up by the water in Lagos. About the marketplace where she bought her favorite fruit, the bright orange-colored African star apple— *agbalumo*. She told her about her husband who had died, and of the terrible times that followed. And about her lively, precocious daughter, Konisola.

"I had to escape," she told Colleen, "for Konisola. I ran for *her* life. I was getting sicker each day. Who would look after her? Who would protect her from Uncle's wrath? Time was running out."

❄ ❄ ❄

"Yes, it's me."

"Konisola, who is there with you?"

"I am alone."

"All alone? When will someone be back?"

"Not until late tonight."

"Konisola, give me the address of where you are. I'm coming to get you."

Colleen's mind races. As a nurse, she's used to thinking fast and dealing with emergencies. But this is an emergency she's never faced before. She has no doubts about picking up the girl. It isn't right that she has been left alone. Colleen knows that Abimbola would want her to try and help. But what will she do with Konisola once she picks her up? Taking her to her own home is out of the question. Colleen is Abimbola's nurse, after all. Nurses don't normally look after their patients' children. And she has two children of her own. What would they say? What would her husband say if she suddenly showed up with a patient's child?

Whenever Colleen is in a pickle, whenever she needs to untangle a problem, she always does the same thing. She calls her friend Darlene. The two have been nurses together for more than twenty years. Colleen had told her all about Abimbola. Darlene had met her too. If anyone could find a solution, it was Darlene.

"There's *nowhere* for her to stay," Colleen explains. "I'm going to get her, but then what?"

"Bring her to my place. She can stay with me for a few days," Darlene offers. "I'll look after her."

"What?" Colleen says. "Are you serious? You would *do* that?"

"Why not? I've got a busy house anyway. What's one more kid for a couple of days?"

TEN

"It worked! It worked!" Konisola races around the apartment excitedly, a spring in her step. She feels like screaming her news from the balcony so that all the children returning from school can hear. "I'm going now! I'm going to be with my mother! *I* have a mother too." She feels something she hasn't felt in weeks. Hope. And the promise of a new beginning. She can almost make believe these last terrible weeks have never happened. *Finally,* she thinks, *we'll start over.* She would forgive her mother for getting sick. Forgive her for sending her away. In that moment, she has forgiven her already.

Konisola wants to be sure to take everything that belongs to her. But she has almost nothing, except for her pile of drawings! She reaches under the mattress and pulls them out. She has kept her promise to herself. A new one each day. She leafs through page after page. The picture of herself and her mother in a park. An airplane. Her own face—a self-portrait.

She looks out the window and waits anxiously.

At last, a knock at the door.

"Konisola?"

She doesn't budge. Another loud knock.

"Konisola, it's me. Colleen. Are you in there? Open the door. It's safe."

ELEVEN

Her eyes travel with the streetlights. Streaks of pink, purple, and fire-orange color the early evening sky.

"Are you taking me to my mom now?" Konisola asks from the backseat of Colleen's car.

"No, not yet. We're going to my friend, Darlene's. She's a nurse on your mother's floor at the hospital. You'll stay with her."

"Darlene?" Konisola chokes. *Who is Darlene? This isn't what I planned.* "But I want to go to my mother."

"The hospital is close by," Colleen says. "You'll be able to visit her often."

Konisola doesn't want to visit her mother. She wants to *stay* with her. She hates the idea of being trapped with another stranger.

They turn onto a wide road lined with homes, some very large and ornate with long walkways and fancy cars. Others, just beside, are tiny and ramshackle. Colleen parks in front of a modest white house. Painted gnomes with red hats decorate the front lawn. The lights are on inside and, through the window, Konisola can see a figure moving about.

As they walk up the front steps, Konisola feels the urge to run. But where to? And how would she ever find her way back to her mother?

The door swings open and a short, red-haired woman stands smiling in front of her.

"You must be *Konnisoola!*" Darlene has a warm smile. Her scratchy voice sounds kind. "Come on in and make yourself comfortable. If you're hungry, I'll fix you something to eat. Ignore the mess. Seems to follow me every-where. I hope Colleen warned you."

As she steps inside, Konisola realizes this is the first time she's ever entered a white person's home. There were people with white skin back home, but not very many, and she didn't know any of them.

"I hear you're gonna be staying with us for a few days," Darlene goes on. "You'll have to teach me how to pronounce your name properly." In her arms, she holds a little boy. He has a round face with red cheeks. "This is my grandson, Kayden. He and my daughter, Sara, live in the basement. Brace yourself. It can get crazy around here!"

Konisola only half-listens. She stands frozen, her eyes fixed on a shadowy figure moving quietly in the background. A slinky black cat stops to stretch and meow. A shiver runs up Konisola's spine.

"And this," Darlene says, "is Princess. She's in charge. She's suspicious at first, but she'll warm to you."

Princess glares at Konisola with gleaming yellow eyes. She yawns and reveals her razor-sharp teeth, whips her tail back and forth. The cat is on high alert. So is Konisola.

Back home, most people she knew were afraid of cats. They weren't house pets. They were wild animals. They could bite you and make you sick.

Konisola is afraid this so-called Princess might pounce at any moment.

"Don't you have a suitcase? Some clothes?" Darlene asks.

Konisola shrugs. "No," she replies, her eyes on the floor.

"She has *nothing*," Colleen says. "Just a couple of small items in this knapsack."

"Nothing?!" Darlene repeats.

Konisola feels her face go hot. "May I go and sit in the parlor?" she asks in the formal English her mother has taught her, the language she insisted Konisola use. Darlene chuckles at the thought of anyone calling her modest living room—with its cat-hair-covered sofa and hand-me-down television stand—a *parlor*.

"I don't have an ice-cream parlor!" Darlene laughs. "I've got two bedrooms and a basement."

"Darlene," Colleen begins, "are you sure this is okay?"

"'Course I am! What's a couple of days? Between my daughter, my grandson, and my big family, I've got people coming and going all the time. Don't forget, I'm a single mom. I'm used to this."

"Okay then. I'll check in tomorrow," Colleen promises and goes out into the night.

Konisola and Darlene stand facing each other in the "parlor." There are a few awkward seconds of silence. Then...

"I have something for you, Konisola," Darlene says. "Dug it up in the basement just before you got here. It belonged to Sara when she was your age. She called it her good luck jacket. I like to think it has a bit of magic. I want you to have it."

It's a light blue jean jacket with an image of a flying girl, a fairy, stitched on the back.

"Tinkerbell," Darlene tells her. "You know, from *Peter Pan?*"

Konisola doesn't know. She eyes the gift. Should she accept it? Would her mother approve?

"Go on," Darlene insists. "Try it on. See if it fits."

Konisola has been wearing the same clothes since she and her mother arrived. She's tired of the thick black pants, the same washed-out long-sleeved T-shirt. It would be wonderful to have something new. Something with a bit of sparkle. Konisola hesitates and then takes the jacket and slips it on. It fits perfectly. It makes her feel older, stronger. And it gives her a feeling: change is coming.

TWELVE

Konisola stares at the cat.

Princess is stretched out on the living room floor, slapping her tail, as if she's keeping watch, standing guard. She licks her paws and rubs the back of her ears. The hairs on the back of Konisola's neck stand up.

"Let's go to the mall," Darlene says. "You're gonna need a few things."

Konisola is frozen.

How, she wonders, *will I get past the cat?*

"Come on, she's actually a lazy old thing. She won't bite. She probably won't even come near you."

Konisola keeps her eyes peeled on Princess, and in small steps, slides out the front door and into the backseat of Darlene's car.

It's evening, but inside the brightly lit mall with neon lights, it feels like high noon. Konisola walks with Darlene, who pushes Kayden in his stroller, past the shiny storefronts bursting with clothes, jewelry, and toys.

There were malls back home, but Konisola had never been inside one. Once a week, she would trail happily behind her mother who, despite the burning sun, seemed to glide through the crowds at the open-air market. Vendors hooted and hollered as they sold their wares—rice and beans, dried chili peppers, avocado, mango, and her mother's favorites, plantain and *agbalumo*, the African star apple. Fish of all shapes and sizes were displayed in slippery, silvery rows.

Stacks of beautiful fabric—blue and yellow,

orange and purple sheets—were folded neatly on shelves. Brightly colored dresses hung from wooden rafters as if suspended from the sky. The air rang with the braided sounds of easy laughter, chatter, and honking car horns. Everywhere, men, women, and even children, balanced large heavy bags and boxes on their heads.

Inside the mall, people rush about in all directions. They eat ice cream, push strollers. They carry glittery boxes and bags. But that's not what catches Konisola's eye. Everywhere she looks, she sees families—arguing, laughing, holding hands. Where is hers?

Darlene buys Konisola some socks and underwear, pajamas, a pair of pants, and a toothbrush. Just enough for a few days.

"We'd better start heading back," Darlene says. They make their way to the parking lot.

Who is that? From a distance, Konisola can

see a young woman leaning against Darlene's car. She's short, with paper-straight strawberry blonde hair that falls to the middle of her back. A freckled face. Jet black fingernails.

"This," Darlene says when they get to the car, "is my daughter, Sara. Sara, meet Konisola."

Konisola squirms uncomfortably.

"You're a lot taller than I expected," Sara says. Sara is fourteen years older than Konisola, but at five feet, not much taller.

"Do you speak English?" Sara asks bluntly.

Konisola wants to answer, to say something, but the words are stuck.

"She speaks it better than we do!" Darlene jumps in. "Okay, gang. Time to get home. Everybody in the car."

"Hang on a sec. Not so fast." Sara reaches into her bag. "This is for you," she says, and hands Konisola a beautiful black doll with thick long hair and eyes that open and close.

Konisola smiles cautiously at Sara. "Thank you."

At home, Darlene shows Konisola to Sara's old bedroom just down the hall from her own.

"You can sleep here. Glad somebody's using it. Holler if you need anything."

"Darlene?" Konisola has to get it out before she loses her nerve. "I need to see my mother."

"Of course you do," Darlene says gently. "You'll come to the hospital with me in the morning. Get some rest now."

Konisola watches the door close. She looks around the small room. The paint-chipped walls covered with posters and photos.

She sits on the edge of the bed with its pink-and-white checkered quilt and examines the gifts—the doll and the denim Tinkerbell jacket. She dreads the thought of going to sleep.

Outside the window, the branches of a solitary tree sway back and forth, casting a moving shadow on the bedroom wall. "Listen to the trees," Teacher often said. "Wise is the one who listens to the trees." *One day, I'll paint that,*

Konisola promises herself. *I'll paint the shadows that dance on the wall in the night.*

She slips under the covers, closes her eyes, and listens to the sounds from the kitchen. The running water and the clanking of dishes. To Darlene humming along to the music on the radio. To anything that might keep her company in the dark.

Darlene seems kind. Still, Konisola can't shake the familiar feeling of aloneness. How has she ended up in yet another stranger's home?

"Tomorrow," she whispers into the quiet of the room. "Tomorrow I'll see her."

THIRTEEN

"STOP!" Konisola screams. Loud, threatening voices. Uncle's face. Her mother's. Konisola feels Uncle's strong hands grab at her, pulling her back into his house.

"Run, Konisola!" her mother yells.

Let me go! She twists her body. But she can't move, can't free herself from Uncle's grip. It's as if her legs are stuck in cement.

"HELP ME! SOMEBODY HELP ME!"

"Konisola," a voice calls. "Konisola." Someone is shaking her. "Wake up. You're having a bad dream."

When she opens her eyes, there's Darlene—her crooked smile, her warm voice, her small hands.

"Everything is okay," she says. "Everything is okay."

Is it? How can *it be?*

FOURTEEN

"What about a piece of toast?" Darlene nudges at breakfast. "Maybe some eggs?"

Konisola looks at all the food on the table. White toast, orange slices, and cereal, but she doesn't touch any of it. She's too jittery to think of food. Her stomach is in a knot.

This is the day. For weeks she's waited and prayed for it. A part of her thought it might never come.

Konisola washes quickly and dresses in the fresh new clothes Darlene bought her the previous night. She wants to look just right when she sees her mother.

Will she be glad to see me? Angry with me for calling Colleen?

"Time to go!" Darlene calls from the kitchen.

Konisola and Darlene enter the sprawling glass and brick hospital. In her hand, Konisola holds the card she made for her mother, from the first picture she sketched, of the two of them in a park.

They pass a big red sign. EMERGENCY. Konisola remembers it from that terrible day when she and her mother ended up there. The loud sounds. The flashing lights. Her mother.

Up the elevator they go. There's a blue-and-white sign on the wall: "6J - Oncology." *What does that mean?* There's a large poster beside the sign, with a photo of a woman with a bald head, an older man, and a young girl. "Cancer Affects Us All," it reads.

Cancer. Konisola knows the word. But not much more.

As they walk, Konisola gags at the stench. The smell of sickness mixed with cleaning solvents. She tries to plug her nose, but it doesn't work. A patient shuffles down the hall, attached to machines that roll alongside. The bright fluorescent lights flicker and make everyone look ghostly.

"Morning, Darlene," a voice calls from the nurses' station.

The doors to most of the rooms are half-open. *So many sick people.* Konisola doesn't want to see them, tries not to look.

At last, Darlene stops. "Here we are."

Konisola bites her lip. Her mother is beyond this door. She has waited for this day. Imagined it. Dreamed of it. Here she is, at last, and she can't move.

She's in there, Konisola thinks to herself. *Just go.* She braces herself and steps inside.

FIFTEEN

Her mother lies in a bed on the far side of the room, just by the window. Is it really *her?* Her eyes are closed. She's thin. She wears a wrinkled, pale blue hospital gown. A string holds it together loosely at the neck. She's attached to tubes and beeping machines. And her hair. All her beautiful hair. It's almost gone. As Konisola approaches, her mother's eyes fly open.

"Oyinkan! You are here."

Konisola drinks in the sound of her mother's voice. At the same time, she wants to run.

"Come closer, my girl," her mother calls. "Let me see your face."

"Mama?" The word that once felt as familiar as her own breath now feels strange coming out of her mouth. A bubble of anger sits in her throat. She can't look her mother in the eye. "Can we leave the hospital now?"

"No. I can't leave yet."

"But you promised. You said we could start over. *I* can take care of you. Let's go outside. I'll walk with you, make you strong, the way you were."

"Not yet, Oyinkan."

And then the questions that had burned in her for so long burst out. "Why did you leave me? Why didn't you come for me?"

"I had no choice. I could not!"

"I want to stay with you. I'll do anything. I can help. I can help make you—"

"You cannot stay here, Konisola. A hospital is not a place for healthy children. The doctors will help me get better. We will be together soon."

SIXTEEN

What now?

When she and Darlene return from the hospital, Konisola hurries to her room and shuts the door. She doesn't want to see or speak to anyone. In her hand, she's still clutching the drawing she made for her mother. She tears it to shreds.

"Konisola?" Darlene knocks, calls softly from the other side of the door. "How about some dinner?"

She doesn't answer.

"You take all the time you need. We'll see your mom again tomorrow."

That night, the nightmares return. They always do. The terrifying scenes, the twists and turns. Her shrieks in the middle of the night.

Darlene returns too.

Konisola was supposed to stay with Darlene for just a few days, but now it's going to be longer.

Darlene and Konisola go back to visit her mother the next day and the day after that. Whenever they can, Konisola and Darlene return to the hospital. Konisola gets the same wobbly feeling in her legs each time she enters the building.

Darlene does what she can to try and make the visits just a little bit easier. "Let's guess which of the elevators is going to open for us." And as soon as they get out on the 6th floor, Darlene hollers, "Never too old to race. First one to your mother's room wins! On your mark. Get set. *Go!*"

Down the long hall they run. Along the way, they pass doctors, nurses, orderlies, and volunteers. Everyone watches them. And Darlene and Konisola are a funny-looking pair. One short and white, jiggly and middle-aged. The other tall and Black, young and strong.

"You got me. This time," Darlene says when they reach Abimbola's room. It's the last one, at the very end.

One evening, they arrive to find Konisola's mother arguing with a nurse.

"No more needles!" her mother says sharply.

Darlene intervenes. "It's for your own good, Abby," she says, using her nickname for Abimbola. "And another thing. You're not going to make many friends that way."

"*Tsk.*" Abimbola clicks her tongue, something she does often when she's annoyed or disappointed. "I am not looking for friends, Darlene. I am trying to get better. I need to get out of here. To be allowed to stay in this country. To be with my daughter!"

Back and forth they go. Neither Darlene nor Abimbola likes to back down.

"We have the same fire in our bellies, Darlene," Abimbola says. "It comes from having raised our children alone and from having looked at death."

❄ ❄ ❄

While the two women talk, Konisola inspects the equipment. She likes the bed's remote control most of all. She examines the heart monitor and the beeping machine. It drips medicine and water through a long plastic tube and needle in her mother's hand. She wants to know about each contraption, each test, each medicine bag, and pill.

Konisola asks many questions at the hospital, of Darlene, of the other nurses and doctors. "How many times does a heart beat?" "What's blood pressure?" "When will my mom's hair grow back?" Each question leads to a new one, and a new one after that.

"You training to be a doctor?" Darlene asks.

Konisola likes that idea. At each visit, she props her mother up, fluffs her pillows, straightens her bed, and carefully helps her turn over. When her mother feels warm, Konisola brings a wet cloth and gently dabs her forehead. When she's cold, she covers her with an extra blanket. The nurses on 6J watch. They watch and shake their heads. "That girl," they say. "She's just like a mother, looking after her own sick mother."

Konisola roams the hospital halls freely. She pokes around the gift shop. Watches movies on a computer in the family lounge. Sometimes, Colleen gives her money for a treat in the cafeteria.

One afternoon, Abimbola is thirsty.

"Bring me some water, Konisola. My mouth is as dry as sand."

Konisola makes her way to the kitchen on

the other side of the hospital floor. Two nurses are seated at a small table. On the counter, a leaning tower of Styrofoam cups. Konisola opens the fridge and picks up the heavy water jug.

"Hello there!" booms a low, gravelly voice.

Konisola jumps. A very tall, older man stands in the doorway. His thick, silver-gray hair is neatly combed. Enormous bushy eyebrows shade his sloping eyes. Friendly eyes, with a hint of sadness in them. A sadness Konisola can recognize.

"There's ice cream in the freezer," he says. Konisola eyes him warily.

"Are you just going to stand there?" he jokes. "Or shall we have some?"

The man opens the freezer, removes two ice-cream cups and hands her one. Konisola can't help but smile when she looks at the wrinkled lines all over his face. *A face like a map.*

They sit together at the table and eat their ice cream in silence. Konisola savors the cool, delicious taste in her mouth. She already wishes for another. When the man is done, he removes a silk handkerchief from his navy jacket and blows his nose—very loudly.

"My name is Willson. I snack here every day at the same time. You're welcome to join me, if you like." And then he stands to leave.

"See you next time, I hope," Willson says.

Next time. She hopes so too.

SEVENTEEN

The arrangement at Darlene's works smoothly enough—at first.

Darlene leaves for work at the hospital each day at the crack of dawn. Konisola stays home with Sara and Kayden. When Darlene returns in the early evening, Sara leaves for her evening job at the mall.

But Konisola still feels awkward and out of place. Everything feels different...*is* different. She's a stranger in a strange land. Sometimes, lonely and at a loss for what to do, she goes to the fridge, pokes her head inside, and tries to find comfort in the food. Once in a while, she receives a food delivery. It begins with a knock at the door. And a familiar voice.

"*Aalo!* Your *fufu* is here!"

Nurse Rita is from Nigeria too. From the same city…Lagos. She's often in Abimbola's hospital room when Konisola comes to visit. Like Colleen, Rita pays special attention to Abimbola. She patiently explains things. Tries to help her with the big decisions about medication, tests, and procedures.

In the middle of the night, when Abimbola is awake worrying about her illness, about the refugee hearing, about the future, about her daughter—Rita comes to her and tries to put her mind at ease.

And every so often, Rita appears at Darlene's house with the Nigerian food that Konisola misses so much. Spicy fish and rice. And *fufu*— an orange sticky dough made with ground yam powder and served with a soup.

When Konisola looks at Rita, when she listens to her voice and her words, she feels a connection. It feels like home.

❄ ❄ ❄

In the beginning, Sara is glad to have another person to play with Kayden. Konisola—an only child—is happy to pretend she has a little brother. It was so lonely in that last empty apartment. It is a huge relief just not being left alone. She teaches Kayden *Tinko Tinko*, a hand-clapping game from home. Sometimes she sits with him on the floor. He colors. She draws.

The three of them visit the library down the street. And the park nearby. Kayden loves the sandpit and the metal slide.

But for Konisola, it's the swings. On a swing, she's in charge. She can pump as hard as she wants, fly as high as her legs can take her. Till the chains jerk. Till she can see over the trees. To Kayden, on the ground, she's queen of the sky.

"Me too!" he yells. "Me too!"

And then one day, "KO-NNIIEEE!"

Konnie. It rolls off the tongue so easily. She loves the breezy sound of her very own nickname. It makes her feel special—like she belongs. The name sticks.

She's been at Darlene's for three weeks, and things are getting complicated.

Kayden is two. There are meltdowns and messes. There's laundry to be done. Cooking and cleaning. And Sara doesn't much like having to do it all. And she doesn't much like having to share her mother and her house with a stranger's child. Her patience is wearing thin.

Konnie doesn't want to be bossed around. She starts lashing out.

The arguments begin.

EIGHTEEN

In her hospital room, Abimbola takes out her red-and-black diary where she addresses her thoughts to her daughter.

Konisola, I want you to go to school. I know you and Darlene want that too. I want you to be somebody in life. You must achieve more than I have. You must be more than I am.

"It's time, Konnie. Your mother and I have talked about this," Darlene says one night at home.

Konnie hasn't been to school for two months. Two months! Since the day she and her mother boarded the plane for Canada. She misses her school friends from back home. She's restless. And lonely for the company of friends her own age.

But school here? Now that she's allowed to go, questions fill her head. *What will the other students be like? Will they talk to me? Will they know more than I do?*

Konnie watches Princess lick a paw. Princess, her new friend, looks back. They have gotten used to each other. Princess sidles up to Konnie, rubs her furry head against Konnie's leg.

NINETEEN

Konnie rubs her hands back and forth on her thighs. Her first day of school in Canada is about to begin. It's the very same school that Darlene attended—and Sara too.

"It'll be good for you," Darlene assures her outside the school office. "I'll pick you up after school. Just this once, because it's your first day." Darlene watches Konisola walk down the corridor and feels a lump in her throat.

Just after 9 a.m., Konnie looks through the window in the door of Room 21. The other students are already seated at their desks, busy and boisterous, laughing and telling jokes before the lessons begin. When Konnie opens the door, everyone stops to look up.

She stands perfectly straight, chin up, at the front of the Grade 4 class.

She feels completely naked.

"Welcome, KON-EE-SO-LA," Mr. Cummings, the teacher, enunciates every syllable carefully.

The students had been told that a new girl would be joining the class. They all stare at Konnie. And Konnie stares back. Some of them have white skin, others are different shades of brown. One has very dark brown skin, as dark as her own. One wears a headscarf.

Konnie tries her best to look confident and strong. Inside, her stomach twists.

Please don't ask me any questions, she prays under her breath. *Please, no questions.*

To Konnie's relief, Mr. Cummings motions for her to take a seat.

The students are grouped in clusters of four.

The girl at the next desk leans over and whispers, "My name is Omara."

Small and nearly half Konnie's size, Omara has light brown skin. Her hair is pulled back off her face and tied tightly in a bun. No other words pass between them that day.

On the field at recess and during lunch, Konnie watches the other students, studying their every move. How they speak to Mr. Cummings—they call him Mr. C.—and to each other.

She watches the games they play, what they say and don't say, the words they use. She wants to use them too. She'll do anything to avoid standing out. She wants to blend in, be part of this new crowd as quickly as she can.

Not so easy.

When Darlene picks Konnie up after school,

her classmates stare. Who is this white woman picking up this Black girl? And the questions begin.

"Is that your babysitter?" a girl asks the next day, and giggles.

"Hey, were you adopted?" a boy yells at her in the schoolyard.

Konnie doesn't know what to say or how to explain who Darlene is. She doesn't want anyone to know her mother is sick. Or that she might be sent back home.

She doesn't answer.

"She's a refugee," a girl says. She makes it sound nasty. Like Konnie's a criminal.

Refugee. There is that word again. *What exactly is a refugee?* Konnie has heard the word many times. At the airport. In the warning from the woman in the apartment. And in the stories about refugees in the news. "*How many is too many?*" "*Are they a threat?*" "*Don't we have room for more?*" And she's heard it most of all in the conversations her mother's had with Darlene and Colleen. *The Refugee Hearing.* It's all her mother seems to think about anymore. Konnie feels a chill each time the subject comes up.

One day at lunchtime, Konnie looks the word up at the school library.

Refugee: Refugees are people who have been forced to leave their homes, their countries, and often their families. They have fled war, violence, conflict, or persecution and have crossed an international border to find safety in another country. They often have to flee with little more than the clothes on their backs.

Konnie and her mother fled violence. They crossed an international border when they moved to the other side of the world. They left *everything* behind. *Why then, is my mother so worried about the hearing? Why wouldn't Canada want us to stay? And how could my mother possibly be sent back if she isn't even strong enough to get out of her hospital bed?*

The bell rings. Lunch is over. Konnie slams the book closed and hurries back to class.

❄ ❄ ❄

"You sure you didn't flunk out of school a few *hundred* times?"

One more thing that makes Konnie stand out—she towers over all the other students. Eddie, the class braggart, whose mouth is in a permanent smirk, won't leave it alone.

Konnie tries to ignore him. But as soon as she climbs on the school bus the next morning and walks past his seat, Eddie sticks his foot out and trips her. He snatches her denim Tinkerbell jacket and jumps on his seat.

"Got it!" he yells. "Betcha can't reach it, giant!"

She can't.

"Oooh…*Tinkerbell!* Look at me, I'm a fairy princess!" Eddie laughs, a hyena's laugh. He waves the jacket around and around his head like a lasso. "You're *very* tall," he jeers. "But *ver-rrry* slow!"

Konnie's blood boils.

"What's the matter, Tinkerbell? I thought you could fly! Come on! Try jumping like yer fat half-mama! I guess your real mother didn't want you!"

Konnie lunges at him. She grabs her jacket and pulls him down with it. Eddie tumbles off his seat and crashes onto the floor of the bus with a loud *thunk*. The other students gawk. A few snicker.

"What! Are you *crazy?*" he hollers. Then quickly, he covers his face with his hand. Blood drips from his nose. "Cantcha take a freakin' joke?!"

Konnie takes her seat and stares out the window. She's shaking. She squeezes her hands tightly around the jacket and rests her forehead against the cold window.

"Next time, get him faster and harder." Omara slips into the seat beside her.

TWENTY

They sit together on the school bus, like two pigeons perched on a wire, their arms almost touching.

Tiny Omara. Even the sound of her name seems perfect to Konnie. And whatever Omara lacks in height, she makes up for in courage. She isn't afraid of anything or anyone.

When Eddie approaches in the schoolyard, Omara turns her hands into claws.

"Take off!" she hollers at him.

And Eddie does.

Brave, tough, funny Omara. She's a bit of a misfit who doesn't quite belong with the other girls or boys in the class. But once she and Konnie find each other, they don't let go. They begin to spend lunchtimes together. Every recess too.

Konnie hasn't told her mother about Omara. She wants to be sure that the friendship is real. But when she looks at Omara, Konnie feels a joy she hasn't felt for a long time. It *has* to be real.

And thank goodness for that.

Because there is no good news from the hospital. Each time Konnie visits her mother, it's a little bit harder. A little bit scarier.

❄ ❄ ❄

The heavy feeling is there again on her next visit.

Konnie takes the elevator to the 6th floor.

On the way to her mother's room, she passes the kitchen. And there's that man. The man with the bushy eyebrows.

"You're back!" Willson's eyes light up. "I

wasn't sure you'd come. Saved you some, just in case."

Konnie cracks a smile. She takes the ice-cream cup from him and sits down to eat. One part of her wants to run to her mother. The other part wants the ice cream—and the visit with Willson. She likes his company, and she likes the sound of his calm, deep voice. He's easy to talk to. He tells her about the work he used to do. She tells him about school.

"Why do you come here?" she asks the man.

"My wife is very sick." He sighs. "She's not getting better. And you? What are you doing here?"

"My mom is sick too." And then Konnie adds quickly, "But she'll be better soon."

TWENTY-ONE

The second Konnie steps into the hospital room, her mother and Nurse Rita stop talking. *What were they saying? What was it they didn't want me to hear?*

"I will leave you now," Rita says to Abimbola. "I'll be back to see you soon."

Konnie detects a hidden message in Rita's voice. It's as if she's speaking in code—and she sees the worry in her mother's eyes.

"Did you study hard today, Konisola?" her mother asks too quickly. Konnie ignores the question and begins to tell her mother about Omara.

"But what about your studies?" her mother presses. "Remember. You must work hard, study, and do well!"

Konnie reaches over to touch her mother's bald head—bald from the cancer treatment. Her mother was always proud of her hair. Konnie loved to twist her fingers through it during the quiet of their late-night talks back home. Now, her mother's head feels smooth and strange.

In bed, her mother places a hand on her stomach, a sign that the pain is bad.

"Remember to say your prayers, Konisola."

She knows she's being dismissed.

TWENTY-TWO

Before she goes to bed, Konnie prays for her mother to get well. She does this each night. And each morning, when she wakes, she marks off yet another day with a big X on the calendar that hangs in her room. Days become weeks, weeks become months, school ends and starts again. Konnie is tired of having her prayers ignored.

Darlene wants to give Konnie something to look forward to. The annual Priestman family reunion might just do it.

Every autumn, on the second weekend in October, the whole crew gathers at the wooden cabin Darlene's dad built with his own hands thirty years earlier. The cabin sits on a wide dark blue lake, surrounded by trees. An old wooden dock juts straight out into the water. Konnie has never seen anything like it. The morning they arrive, there are three deer standing stock still in a forest clearing just off the road to the cabin.

"*Shhhhh*," Darlene whispers. "Don't move. Don't make a sound." The deer stop, look up, and quickly bound off into the woods. Konnie can't wait to tell her mother and Omara.

"I'm glad you're here celebrating with us," Darlene tells Konnie. "Gets my mind off missing my dad so much. This is our first family reunion without him."

Inside the cabin, Konnie comes to a standstill, overwhelmed by the amount of noise. Darlene comes from a big, boisterous family. She has a straight-talking, piano-playing mother and a pile of nieces, nephews, aunts, and uncles. Five sisters and brothers.

A huge man approaches. "Konnie, meet my brother Greg," Darlene says. Greg towers over Darlene. A giant with a heart of gold was how Darlene described him. Greg is six feet tall, burley as a bear, and has a completely shaven head. He's wearing what he calls his suit: ripped jeans and a ragged old sweatshirt.

"Would it have killed you to shower and change?" Darlene jabs him in the arm.

"You going fancy on me now, Darlene?" He looks at Konnie. "My sister likes to razz me. Would you believe I've got two other sisters to match? Each one, five feet tall, five feet 'round. Love 'em to bits." Then he bends down, *way* down, to give Darlene a tight hug. "Konnie, you make sure to call me *Uncle* Greg."

Uncle Greg. Konnie likes him already. Uncle Greg. So different from the uncle she knew.

Konnie sees Sara across the room, scowling, eyeing her coldly. Konnie senses the anger. Has she done something wrong?

Around the dinner table, everyone tells

funny stories about Darlene's dad. Konnie doesn't know all the characters, she doesn't get all the inside jokes, but she watches closely and listens and loves every minute of it. She can almost make believe she belongs here. Make believe she is one of them.

TWENTY-THREE

It's late at night when they return home. The cat is waiting for them.

"Hi Princess." Konnie kneels down to stroke her. Then she goes to her room and closes the door. Exhausted and happy, she gets under the covers, still in her sweatshirt. She places her face in the crook of her arm and breathes in the scents from her sleeve—pine and cedar, roasted marshmallows, and burning wood from the fireplace. She wants to hold on to the smell of the weekend for as long as she can.

She almost falls asleep, but a hushed and

heated conversation erupts in the living room. And Konnie can hear every word.

"How long is this gonna go on for, Mom?" Sara hisses. "Konnie was only supposed to be here for a couple of days, remember? That was ages ago!"

"Sara, the doctors are doing their best. I know it's not easy for you."

"Not *easy?*" Sara says. "I'm busy looking after Kayden all day *and* doing laundry. *And* preparing food. *And* working evenings. Now I'm looking after someone else's kid too! You gave her my old room, my old clothes. *Everything.* You never even asked me. I feel badly for her too, Mom, but sometimes I feel like you're forgetting about *me.* About me and Kayden."

Konnie gets out of bed. She crouches on the bedroom floor, knees to her chest, ear to the door.

"I know she's just a kid. I know her mom's in the hospital," Sara continues. "I keep saying to myself, *something good will come of it.* But it's gotten to be too hard. I feel like she's taking over our lives. And she argues with me about *everything*. What to eat. When to leave the house. When to come back. When to clean up. I'm ready to quit, Mom. I'm honestly ready to quit."

"She has *no one*, Sara. No one, and nowhere else to go. They're still waiting for their refugee hearing. They don't even know *if* they'll be allowed to stay. Please, be patient. Just a little longer."

Konnie feels as if the air is being sucked out of her lungs. She thinks back to all the arguments she's had with Sara. They happened most often when Darlene was at work. Sara expected Konnie to listen. And in the early days she did. But just like Sara, she's fed up. Sick of taking orders. Sick of her mother still being in hospital.

One afternoon last week, there was another flare-up.

"Pick up your art supplies, Konnie! Get them off the living room floor. Kayden will eat them!" Sara yelled for the tenth time.

"Leave me alone!" Konnie shouted back angrily. "You're not my mother!" She pushed past Sara, ran to her room, and slammed the door.

"Yeah, well, you're not my kid!" Sara growled. "And I don't need this."

TWENTY-FOUR

Konnie wishes she could take all her angry words back, erase all the arguments. *What if they send me away?*

Then…another thought.

Maybe I should just go.

In the middle of the night, Konnie is frantic. She doesn't have a plan. But she knows she needs to do something. *I'm not wanted here. I have to get away.* She squishes a pair of leggings, some fresh underwear, and a sweatshirt into her school knapsack. She hesitates at her Tinkerbell jacket—*Sara's* Tinkerbell jacket, the one that was supposed to bring her luck—and leaves it on the chair.

Everyone is sound asleep. Everyone except Princess, who sits on the windowsill. Eyes and ears alert, she raises her head and stares at Konnie.

"*Shhhh*," she whispers and closes the front door behind her.

On the sidewalk, Konnie stops, turns around, and looks back at the house. Her heart hurts. Her bones feel cold. All is quiet. *Now what?*

She has an idea. Konnie moves cautiously along the deserted streets. She keeps her eyes peeled on the roads. She has never walked alone at night. Just when she thinks it can't get any darker, it grows darker still. And then she thinks she hears footsteps. Is someone—or something—following her? Konnie's chest throbs. She is dizzy with fear. And then she realizes the footsteps are her own. Her own shadow and movements have spooked her.

Why is it taking so long? Isn't this the same

route she has taken with Sara and Kayden many times before? Konnie searches for a familiar sign, something, anything to let her know she's headed in the right direction. Maybe she should have waited just a few more hours, until the early morning light.

But there's no turning back now. Shivering and scared, she keeps going.

Soon, some of the trees and homes begin to look familiar. The red-and-white mailbox too. She's sure that's the one they always pass, with graffiti all over it. But where is the path with the crabapple trees?

At last, in the distance, she sees it—a sliver of moonlight shimmers on the metal slide. She runs to the slide and to her swing. She climbs on and rocks back and forth. The rusting metal chains squeak with each glide.

It starts to rain, spitting at first, and then falling in sheets. There's a small wooden hut in the playground that Kayden likes to pretend is his house. She makes a run for it.

Inside, she sits on the gravel and leans against the wall. It smells of wood and wet sand. It smells of loneliness and fear. Konnie trembles—from the cold and from all the not knowing.

And her stomach is rumbling. She's hungry and thirsty. In the rush to get out, she didn't think to bring food or a flashlight. She digs into her knapsack, feeling her way around, and pulls out a cookie left over from last Friday's lunch. She eats slowly, nibbling, hoping to make it last.

She thinks of her new friends, Omara and Willson. She thinks of Darlene, who comes to her in the middle of the night when she has those awful dreams. And she thinks of Sara's words—*she's taking over our lives.*

Outside, the wind blows. Brown leaves rustle along the ground. Raccoons screech and snarl and whimper. Konnie listens to the mysterious sounds of the night. Then, a crack in the sky, a clap of thunder, and the rain hammers on the roof of the hut. She wishes morning would come.

"If you see the sun and the rain at the same time," her mother told her late one night back home, "it means the lion is giving birth." Alone in the dark, damp hut, Konnie would give anything for the morning light.

But for now, all she can do is listen to the steady rhythm of the rain. She struggles to keep her eyes open and then gives in and lets them rest. *I'll close them…just for a second.*

Konnie sleeps.

Until she hears a frantic cry.

TWENTY-FIVE

"Konnie! KONNNNEEE! If you're here, please answer me! If you can hear me, PLEASE. Come out! I'M SORRY. I DIDN'T MEAN WHAT I SAID."

Konnie looks through an opening of the hut. She peers outside and stares. There is Sara, yelling frantically. Her face is red and streaked from crying. Konnie takes a tiny step, just a few inches. Sara sees her peeking out. She runs to her, takes Konnie in her arms, and holds her close.

"I'm so sorry, Konnie. For all the things I said. My whole life, it was always just me and my mom. The two of us. Then I had Kayden and we became a threesome. I thought it would stay that way. As crazy as it sounds, I thought I'd always have my mom to myself." She looks at Konnie. "I feel awful, Konnie—I'm the adult. I didn't mean what I said." They sit on the wet ground, rocking back and forth. "Promise me you'll never disappear like that again."

Konnie is silent. She clings tightly to Sara.

Konnie says nothing to her mother about the incident. She hopes Darlene won't either. She wants, *needs,* everything to be right.

Sara is extra nice to her after that, lets her stay up a bit later than before, tries not to raise her voice when she's frustrated.

Konnie tries hard to control her own temper. Tries to remember to pick up her things. She offers to help with Kayden more often. She tries to let Sara and Darlene have some alone time.

Konnie and Darlene keep up their visits to the hospital. And Abimbola receives the date for their refugee hearing. Hers and Konnie's.

January 26. Unbelievable. It's Konnie's birthday. Nine weeks away. Nine weeks until they find out if they can stay or if they'll be forced to leave.

When Konnie asks Darlene—as she often does—how much longer Abimbola will have to stay in the hospital, she never seems to get a straight answer.

And then one night, Darlene doesn't answer at all. Darlene tries to smile at her, but it turns out crooked and sad, and then she changes the subject.

Konnie feels something shift under her feet. It isn't a good feeling.

Sometimes, Konnie doesn't know what to do with all her bad feelings. Some days, she just feels like crying. On other days, even though she wants to be on her best behavior, she has a powerful urge to kick the wall. To scream. There are times when Darlene is called to the school in the middle of the day because of Konnie's anger.

So once a week after school, Konnie begins to get together with a woman named Mehr. "Rhymes with care," she tells Konnie. Mehr has long silver hair that looks like waves of tinsel. She wears dangling earrings. She has a rich, deep voice. And her hands and clothes are always paint-splattered.

The room they meet in is big and bright with large windows. There are tubes of paint in every color. Glass jars hold water and brushes, colored pencils and markers.

Konnie and Mehr each have a rickety wooden easel. They spend most of their time together painting. But Mehr always has questions.

"How's school?"

"Fine."

"I hear you ran away."

Silence.

"Want to talk about it?"

"No."

"Want to tell me about your last visit with your mother?" Mehr continues.

"It was okay."

Okay. Fine. Code for "I don't want to talk about it." That's how Konnie answers all questions about her mother. What is there to say? That she doesn't know how any of this happened? That she's scared and mad and confused?

"Want to make something for her?" Mehr asks.

"Like what?"

"How about a shawl? Something to comfort her, keep her warm?"

Together, Konnie and Mehr dig through the storage room and collect piles of fabric and art supplies. Mehr teaches Konnie how to thread a needle and sew a simple stitch. And they begin to string together swaths of cotton, canvas, and muslin that Konnie paints.

Pomegranate red.

Burnt orange.

Sunflower yellow.

Ultramarine.

Lilac.

One afternoon, Konnie places the large sheet they've made on the ground and lies on top of it, face up, arms outstretched. Mehr traces Konnie's outline to reveal her shape. Konnie dips her palms in a plate of blue paint, stamps them all over the fabric. A crisp ultramarine.

"The most prized blue," Mehr tells her. "It means, 'beyond the sea.' At one time, this pigment was costlier than gold. Too costly for Michelangelo."

Each week, Konnie throws herself into the project. She loves the sewing, the gluing, the painting. There's magic in the making, in the doing. She's doing something for her mother. And that feels so good.

TWENTY-SIX

"Can my mom come to the party too?"

It's December. Christmas is just around the corner. It'll be Konnie's first. Darlene's family plans to gather for a big feast. Konnie, Darlene, Sara, and Kayden pick out a tree. Konnie can't wait for the holiday. But she hates the thought of her mother stuck in a hospital bed while everyone else celebrates.

"I don't know, Konnie. Might be too risky. Let me ask her doctors."

"Please, Darlene," she begs. "*Pleeease* make them say yes!" She spends the last week before

Christmas thinking of nothing else. In school, she doesn't hear a word Mr. C. says.

On Christmas Eve, Konnie plants herself in front of the living room window.

She counts the minutes. The food is ready. Darlene's raucous family has already started to arrive. And still no sign.

Then Konnie hears the sputtering sounds, and seconds later, Darlene's small beige car pulls into the driveway. Konnie runs to the front door and sees Darlene get out of the car. Alone. *What about my mother? Did something go wrong?*

The door opens on the passenger side. A head appears in the backseat, a familiar head with a blue-and-yellow scarf. *She is here! She made it!* Darlene helps Konnie's mother pull herself, slowly, painfully, into a wheelchair.

"Send me those good-for-nothing brothers of mine!" Darlene hollers to Konnie.

And out they come. Uncle Greg, head shaved, in his regular "suit"—ripped jeans and an old T-shirt. And Trevor, his opposite. Soft-spoken. Blond. Neatly dressed in pants and a button-down shirt. Both so tall, the giants in the family. Together, the brothers roll Abimbola in her wheelchair toward the house. They hoist the chair, and its precious passenger, over the concrete steps one at a time. Abimbola smiles. Konnie holds her breath.

One. Two. Three. Four. *At last.*

Konnie lets out a sigh of relief.

Her mother is here. And, for once, she isn't wearing the drab hospital gown. Darlene went early to help Abimbola change. Now she's wearing her traditional Nigerian clothes: a long blue-and-yellow dress with a matching scarf wrapped around her head.

"Wow, Mama," Konnie exhales. "You look like a queen."

Family and friends squeeze into Darlene's house. The dining room table is piled high with food. Roast turkey and stuffing, cranberry sauce, mashed potatoes with gravy. And in honor of Konnie and her mother, Nigerian favorites that Rita has delivered. *Moi moi*—black-eyed beans with spicy fish. Rice and tomato stew. And not to be missed, fufu with yam powder. Hot sauce on all of it. Nothing is ever spicy enough.

"Easy, Konnie. You're gonna fry your insides!" Darlene warns.

After the feast, everyone sits around the tree opening gifts. Konnie places a purple paper crown on top of her mother's headscarf. She wishes this night could last.

Konnie points her brand-new camera—the one Darlene gave her that night—at her mother, focuses the lens on her long, beautiful face. Her tired eyes. Her tall forehead. Her thick, rounded lips.

She snaps the photo.

Abimbola looks at all the white faces around the room, listens to the deep belly laughs, the inside jokes. No one here looks like her, sounds like her. But her daughter is happy. Kayden curls up on Konnie's lap, squirming and laughing as she tickles him. It's as if Konnie has been here forever.

Konnie feels herself being watched. She looks up and sees the pools of tears in her mother's eyes.

At the end of the evening, Darlene's brothers lift Abimbola once more. They carry her to the car and drive her back to the hospital.

That night, before she gets into bed, Konnie sits at her desk and draws a picture. Of her mother wearing a crown.

❋ ❋ ❋

At the hospital, alone once more in her room, Konnie's mother takes out pen and paper too. Every word she writes takes a huge effort.

If anything happens to me, I wish for my daughter, Konisola, to remain in the care of Darlene Priestman.

She signs and dates the letter. Folds it. Places it in an envelope, and licks it closed. She tucks it between the pages of her red diary.

TWENTY-SEVEN

"What if they try to send Konisola back?"

Konnie freezes. She's standing in the hall, outside her mother's hospital room. But she can hear her mother's voice, thick with panic. An expert in the art of eavesdropping, Konnie hides behind the door but carefully leans in to watch and listen.

Wild-eyed, her mother grabs Darlene's hand. "*This* is where Konisola's life is now. *This* is where she must remain! I have to prepare for the worst, Darlene. No matter what happens to me, and no matter what happens at the refugee hearing, Konisola must never return to her uncle's home. *Never!*"

Konnie and her mother were allowed to enter Canada, but that doesn't mean they'll be allowed to stay. In two weeks' time, they'll have to prove to a member of the Immigration and Refugee Board that they *need* to stay. That it's a matter of life and death.

Darlene tells Abimbola that she'll do everything she can to help.

The surgery that might help Abimbola has been put off so that she can attend the hearing. She has to be there in person to plead their case and state her wishes.

But Darlene knows there are no guarantees. Abimbola is living on borrowed time and the decision could go either way.

There's a lot of work to be done.

Forms to be filled out, appointments to be kept, doctors to see.

Like all refugee applicants, Konnie will have to undergo a full medical examination. It will have to be done by a doctor who has experience with refugees and is on a special list.

They sit together, Konnie and Darlene, in the small examination room. There's a high table covered with crisp white paper. A poster of the human body. A scale with an extendable metal measuring stick. Konnie has watched doctors and nurses examine her mother many times. Now it's her turn, and she wants to run.

But Dr. Anna Banerji is exactly what they need. A children's doctor who specializes in refugee health. She understands how serious the hearing is and what's at stake for Konnie.

Dr. Banerji speaks quickly and asks questions about Konnie's health and her mother's. She checks Konnie's eyes, ears, nose, and skin. She feels around her abdomen, taps on her knees, weighs and measures her, takes her blood pressure, and checks her heartbeat with a stethoscope. Konnie gags when the doctor places a large wooden Popsicle stick on her tongue. The doctor makes notes.

When the check-up is over, the doctor sits down to type a letter.

"What does it say? What does it say?!" Konnie pleads with Darlene as soon as they're outside.

Darlene unfolds the page and begins to read aloud.

To the Immigration and Refugee Board,

I examined Konisola—a refugee claimant—in my Refugee Health Clinic today.

On examination, Konisola is healthy with a normal physical exam. There is no known significant past medical history. She has not complained of any fevers, weight loss, or failure to thrive. Her energy level is high, and she has a very good appetite.

Konisola's father died in Nigeria some years ago. Konisola and her mother went to live with her uncle who was apparently very abusive to them, with the abuse resulting in Konisola's mother being hospitalized in their country.

Konisola's mother is in hospital being treated for advanced stage colon cancer. I fear for Konisola's safety and feel strongly that if she is returned to her uncle's home, her life and health would be at risk.

Please do not hesitate to contact me if you have any questions.

Anna Banerji, MD

Will it be enough?

"Darlene?" Konisola asks. "Am I going to be sent away?"

TWENTY-EIGHT

"Where were you this morning?" Omara asks Konnie.

The two don't go straight home from school that afternoon.

They're walking, instead, toward the train tracks. Just below, there's a long concrete tunnel. They step inside.

Hands cupped around their mouths, they call to each other and listen to the sound bounce back.

"Omara!"

"Konnie!"

They run, hand in hand, to the nearby ravine and its rushing stream.

"My mother'll kill me if I get wet!" Omara hollers. Mouth wide, teeth exposed, her laugh is full and loud.

The two friends sit together on the bank, between two giant rocks. "This will be our spot," they decide. "Our secret spot."

"Well, where were you this morning?"

Konnie tosses some small stones into the water. Omara is the truest, strongest friend she's ever had. But Konnie doesn't want to say where she's been. She doesn't want to have to tell her that she might not be around much longer. That one day soon she might simply vanish.

TWENTY-NINE

At 8:00 a.m. on January 26, the three of them—Darlene and Konnie and Abimbola in her wheelchair—enter the elevator of the tall metal-clad building at 74 Victoria Street. Up on the fourth floor, the sign reads:

IMMIGRATION AND REFUGEE BOARD.

They approach the glass-enclosed reception area. While her mother and Darlene speak to a young woman behind the first window, Konnie looks around the crowded waiting room. So many people, speaking in languages she's never heard before. *Is everyone here a refugee?*

A young man stands in a corner. He's skinny and disheveled. His face is unshaven. He looks as if he's been wandering for years. He glances up at the TV screen, the one that lists the room numbers and times for each hearing. Over on the other side of the room, a woman in a striped top and a brown hat speaks nervously into her cell phone. She keeps rubbing her face, her eyes zig-zagging across the room, searching frantically. A family—a mother, father, and four young children—are huddled together. They speak in hushed tones. The mother wears a navy headscarf, her dress nearly reaches her ankles. She holds the youngest on her lap, a little girl in a bright pink jumper, her cheek pressed against her mother's chest. At the back, Konnie sees a boy about her age. He sits alone. No parents. No family.

Most of all, Konnie sees the fear in the room. She feels it too. *What are they running from?* she wonders. *And how many will be allowed to stay? Will I? What if the application is denied? What if they say no?*

Konnie's mother grips her side and winces. She's in a lot of pain.

"Konisola." Her mother motions for her to sit very close. Their faces are almost touching. "No matter what they decide today," her mother whispers urgently in her ear, "no matter what they say, and no matter what happens to me, you *cannot* go back to live under Uncle's roof." She removes a white envelope from her bag. There are documents. And there's some money too. She seals the envelope and places it firmly in Konisola's hands.

"Do not open it until you must. It is all we have."

Their number is called. Room Three, 8:45 a.m. Konnie flinches. It's all happening too fast. She needs everything to stop moving. But there's no way out, no way to stop what has already begun.

Darlene rolls Abimbola's wheelchair slowly forward. Her fists are clenched. Her breathing shallow and raspy. Even seated. The slightest move is almost unbearable.

"Abby," Darlene says softly. "Maybe we should ask to postpone the hearing. You're too weak. Maybe this isn't a good idea."

"No!" she answers sharply. "We must do this. *Now*. There is no time to waste." She straightens her neck, lifts her chin, and stares straight ahead.

Konnie can't help but wonder if they're doomed. Her mother's words circle in her head. *No matter what happens to me. No matter what they decide today...*

The narrow hallway is lined with private hearing rooms, a number is posted above each one.

Number three. The room, with its bare walls, feels cold. A Canadian flag hangs from a pole in the corner. There are rectangular tables. A microphone sits on each one. Everything is being recorded.

The board member in a dark suit is small and stern-looking. She inspects them over her reading glasses from a large wooden desk. She leans forward and speaks into her microphone.

"Introduce yourselves by name, one at a time, please, beginning with the applicant."

"My name is Abimbola. This is my daughter, Konisola. And this is our close friend and nurse, Darlene Priestman."

"Konisola will have to identify herself," the board member corrects.

"My name is Konisola," she says softly.

"Louder please," the decision-maker instructs.

"My name is Konisola," she repeats a bit louder. "But everyone calls me Konnie now."

Darlene rubs and squeezes her own hands anxiously.

"I'm Darlene Priestman. I'm here as Abimbola's nurse. She has special medication that I have to administer. I promised the hospital I would be with her at all times."

Darlene leans over and confesses quietly to Konnie. "Feels like I've been called into the principal's office for detention." She gives Konnie's arm a squeeze.

Abimbola begins. She has been instructed to provide details of what happened to them. To give only the facts.

She recounts their story, the one she has repeated many times before.

Of her dead husband, Konnie's father.

Of his brother.

Of the terrible violence.

The bruises. The broken ribs. The concussion. The black eye. The cuts and the swollen lip. The threats to her life and to Konnie's. Darlene closes her eyes.

Abimbola has the police report from home.

A letter from the hospital in Nigeria where she was treated for her injuries. The letter about Konisola from Dr. Banerji.

The decision-maker asks questions. Konnie's mother answers each one. To Konnie, the minutes feel like days.

"I love my home country," Abimbola says, her voice trembling. "But my daughter's life is in danger!" Her mother's urgent, pleading voice cuts through the air. And then she stops. There's a deafening silence.

"I ran away to protect *her*. Send me back if you must. But *please, let my daughter stay!*"

"One final question. What will happen to Konisola if you don't get better? Who will take care of her then?"

Konnie's insides splinter.

If.

Darlene knows all could be lost in an instant. There's no time to think. Without missing a beat, she jumps in. "She'll stay with me, your honor…Madam. I'll take care of her." The words fly unbidden out of her mouth. *Good Lord,* she thinks to herself, *what have I just said?*

"I will reserve my decision," the member announces. "The Refugee Protection Division will send you my written answer."

THIRTY

During the car ride back to the hospital, no one speaks. They are exhausted and scared. They had hoped for an immediate answer. No one knows what to say or think. Did it go well? They have no idea.

Before returning to Abimbola's room, they stop at the hospital cafeteria. Konnie pulls open the door.

"Surprise! Happy Birthday, Konnie!"

Konnie gasps. They're all there. Sara and Kayden. Darlene's mom. Colleen. Several doctors and nurses from 6J. Rita. There are balloons and streamers. And at the head of the table, a

131

cake that Darlene has baked, with the words *Happy Birthday Konnie!*

There are gifts too. A new knapsack. A set of art supplies with pastels, watercolor paints, a sketchbook. And a silver necklace with a wishbone, one more good luck charm for Konnie. These are her gifts for turning ten.

Colleen snaps a photo on her phone—of Konnie smiling.

Her mother is in a wheelchair on her left. Darlene is standing behind, arms around Konnie.

❈ ❈ ❈

Six days later, a letter arrives in the mail. *This has to be it. The letter we've been waiting for.* Konnie recognizes the typed return address. She holds the white envelope up to the light, tries to see the words. Anything. The answer is in there, she knows it. The words that will decide her future.

When she and Darlene arrive at the hospital,

Colleen is already in her mother's room. They stand together, huddled at the edge of Abimbola's bed and watch, hearts racing, as she tears open the envelope.

Abimbola lets out a cry.

The Refugee Protection Division determines that the claimants are Convention refugees and therefore the Refugee Protection Division accepts your claims.

Abimbola lifts the letter to her lips and kisses the page. The answer they had hoped and prayed for.

They can stay.

THIRTY-ONE

With the refugee hearing behind them, Abimbola can finally have the surgery she needs. She knows it's her last chance at a cure. It's scheduled for Friday. It will be a big and complicated operation. Konnie is relieved it's happening. Finally, she hopes, they'll make her mother better.

Her mother is hopeful too. She prays she'll get well, believes she will. In her diary, she writes:

I have faith that this will work. They will remove the cancer from my body, and I will be with my child.

❄ ❄ ❄

That morning, a quick hug. A quick squeeze of the hand, and her mother is rolled away on a stretcher.

Konnie and Darlene sit together in the tiny waiting room.

The time passes *so* slowly. Konnie and Darlene try to stay busy. They play cards, eat in the cafeteria, go to the hospital gift shop, and buy her mother some yellow carnations.

"Darlene? Why is this taking so long?"

"They're being extra careful. Doing the best they can."

When her mother is finally returned to her room, she's still drowsy. Konnie doesn't want to leave her side.

"I'm staying here till she wakes up," she tells Darlene.

Konnie plants herself in the chair beside her mother's bed. She stares at Abimbola—her thin eyebrows, her sharp cheekbones, the tiny dent in her chin—the one no one else knows about or would even notice. Watching her mother sleep used to be one of Konnie's favorite things in the world. Used to be. Not anymore. Now, when she looks at her mother, she wishes she would wake up, talk to her, tell her everything will be okay.

Abimbola sleeps through the afternoon, until the sun goes down.

"Are you better now, Mama?" Konnie asks when her mother finally opens her eyes. "Did the surgery work?"

Abimbola smiles sleepily but doesn't answer.

❄ ❄ ❄

In the days that follow, Konnie stops asking. She already senses the answer in the faces of those around her. The awkward smiles. The long faces. And she hears it in the hushed tones. Bits and pieces of conversation between Darlene and Colleen, between Darlene and her mother.

Konnie keeps her ears open and alert at all times. The truth, she knows, lives in the whispers, always in the whispers. In what she isn't supposed to hear.

"What's best?"

"Are you sure?"

"Prepare Konnie."

THIRTY-TWO

"Come closer, Oyinkan." Her mother motions for her to sit beside the bed. Konisola bristles at the somber but clipped tone of her mother's voice. She stares at her mother's tired eyes, at her cracked lips, at her almost see-through skin.

"Oyinkan, I am very sick. The doctors say I will not live much longer."

Stop! Make her stop! Konnie doesn't want to hear another word. "You *can*—"

"No, Konisola." Her mother interrupts her. "Listen carefully. You are free now, to be somebody, to live your own full life. Here. And you must be courageous."

Courage? How can I be strong and brave when my mother is dying? Konisola doesn't feel strong at all. Instead, she feels gut-wrenching terror.

"You lied!" Konnie screams. "You promised to get better. To start over! You promised to live!"

Konnie's chest tightens around itself. Her throat fills with stones. She doesn't want to cry. Not here. Not now. She tears out of her mother's room and runs. She runs past the other patients' rooms, past the nurses' station, down the long hall, and through a door. She runs down one flight of stairs and then another…until her legs give way. She drops down onto the cold, hard floor and the tears pour out.

Her worst fears are coming true. How can she live in a world without her mother? Even if their lives have been hard and scattered. Even if her mother is lying in a hospital bed. At least she's alive.

Konisola lies on the ground, head throbbing. She doesn't move. She doesn't hear. Not even the sound of the footsteps approaching from behind.

When Darlene sits down on the floor beside her, Konnie doesn't look up. She knows it's her. She knows it without even opening her eyes.

❄ ❄ ❄

At school, Konnie sits in class. But often she doesn't hear the lesson. Her mind is elsewhere.

After school, whenever they can, Konnie and Omara go to their special spot in the ravine. They sit together on their favorite rock and throw stones and twigs into the cold rushing water.

Konnie wants to tell Omara what's happening to her mother. But she doesn't know how to do it. Each time the words are on the tip of her tongue, she swallows them. In class the next day, she tears off a piece of lined paper from her notebook and writes:

My mother is dying.
If I disappear, please come find me.
Your friend,
Konnie.

She folds the note.
On top, in black marker: **OPEN TONIGHT**.

Almost at the same moment, Abimbola writes a
quote in her diary.

Your present circumstances do not determine
where you go, they merely determine where
you begin.

THIRTY-THREE

"Will you keep her? Will you adopt my child?"

The next day, Abimbola and Darlene are alone in the hospital room.

"Darlene, I am asking you to be a mother to my child. To make her yours…permanently."

"Are you sure this is what you want, Abby? You and I come from completely different worlds. Lots of people will say Konnie should be raised by family, not by strangers. Or by a Black family, not by a short, white, red-headed single woman."

"You are right, Darlene. Maybe if you were Nigerian. Or Black. Or Muslim. Maybe if you were any one of these, it *would* be better. Easier."

She places a hand on her aching stomach and closes her eyes for an instant. "But as my grandmother used to say, 'Look for perfection and you will look forever. And still, forever will not come.' I do not have forever. I have only weeks.

"I believe we were brought together, Darlene. My grandmother taught me about *Ubuntu*—an African idea, 'I am because you are.' You have cared for Konisola all this time. And you asked for nothing in return. You fed my child, clothed her, sent her to school. Tended to her in the night. You love her. And she loves you too. You are the one to care for Konisola. I see it as clearly as I see you now."

Darlene listens but says nothing. She knows decisions have to be made quickly about Konnie's future, but no words come. She doesn't know what to say. She loves Konnie. *But...to raise another child, now? At my age? I already have a grown daughter. And a grandson. And an elderly mother. What would they say? They would say this is crazy.* She could hear them already: *Are you nuts? Are you out of your mind?*

They would say all that and more.

And maybe they're right. Maybe. Darlene thinks back to that first night, more than eight months ago. Konnie on her doorstep. Scared. Disheveled. Alone. With nothing. It was just supposed to be for a couple of days.

If she isn't going to adopt Konnie, who will?

"Darlene, this isn't for a few months, or even a few years. This is *a lifetime*," Colleen says that afternoon in the hospital cafeteria. "If you adopt her, that's it. Is this really what you want? Darlene, you don't *have* to keep her. No one will think badly of you if—"

Darlene lifts up her hand, signaling for her friend to stop. "I've made up my mind. I'm doing this because I can. Because I want to. Konnie has been through too much already.

How could I give her up to Children's Aid *now?* I could never live with myself. I *know* Konnie. I know what foods she likes. What to pack her for lunch. How to soothe her in the night. I know her favorite colors, who her friends are, the games she likes to play. Konnie is a part of me now. I'm just as attached to her as she is to me. I believe I was led to this, Colleen. I was meant to do this."

In her hospital room, Abimbola writes in her red diary:

Konisola, I love you so much. I want you to be a good daughter to Darlene. She's the only one I trust to take care of you. I don't want you to live with anyone else.

It is her final entry.

THIRTY-FOUR

"Say something Konnie. Anything," Darlene pleads.

It's no use. Konnie isn't speaking.

In the evenings, Darlene tries to coax her out of her room, to watch a movie, play cards, talk. Nothing works. Konnie feels betrayed. And angry. At her mother. At Darlene. At the world.

"You don't have to keep me," she spits out one night when she and Darlene are in the car coming home from the hospital. She glares out her side window, tries to keep her face hidden. She doesn't want Darlene to see her eyes welling up.

Darlene pulls the car over and stops at the side of the road. "I know I don't *have* to, Konnie. I *want* to." Darlene pauses. "I always prayed for a second child. And here you are."

Late at night, when Sara gets back from work, Konnie hears the front door open and close. Darlene is leaving for the hospital. She's going to visit Abimbola, to keep her company, to give her comfort, and hold her hand. She does this almost every night now.

"Darlene," Abimbola says, "we are sisters now."

Darlene doesn't tell anyone about her late-night visits. And she doesn't tell anyone about the envelope in the bottom drawer of her bedroom dresser. Once a month, after she receives her paycheck from work, Darlene takes a little bit of money—she doesn't have much to spare—and places it in the envelope. She knows the day will come when Konnie will want to visit Nigeria, the country she came from, the country her mother loves.

"When she's ready," Darlene promises herself, "we'll visit together."

It is decided.

Darlene will first apply for custody, to become Konnie's legal guardian, responsible for her care. This has to happen while Abimbola is still alive, while she can clearly state her wishes. After that, Darlene will apply for adoption.

A court date is set. May 9. They have two months to prepare.

Darlene needs legal advice. She contacts a string of lawyers.

"Too busy," says one.

"Too difficult," says another.

"Too complicated."

"Too expensive."

The lawyers see only the obstacles. Refugees. A sick mother. A single mother, not related. Darlene's heart sinks with each rejection. But she refuses to give up. She'll appear in court on her own if she has to.

Each evening after work and after a visit to the hospital, Darlene sits at the kitchen table and researches "Custody and Adoption Laws." She searches and reads and takes notes.

Konnie often falls asleep to the sound of Darlene *tap*, *tap*, *tapping* on the keyboard. One morning she wakes to find Darlene still at the table, her eyes bloodshot. She slumps over, puts her head in her hands.

"I'm sorry, Konnie, I don't know what I'm doing. I'm a nurse, not a lawyer!"

Konnie suddenly remembers something. She looks at Darlene and a small smile creeps over her face. "I know a lawyer," she says.

THIRTY-FIVE

It's something of a miracle.

Because right there, on 6J, on the very same floor where Darlene works and where Konnie's mother lies dying, is Willson. Willson, Konnie's gray-haired ice-cream friend. Willson, a retired lawyer now caring for his very sick wife.

And Willson isn't just any retired lawyer. He was once the Children's Lawyer of Ontario. A lawyer whose job it was to help protect children. To stand up for them when no one else could or would.

One afternoon, Darlene tells Willson their story.

"I've seen a lot in my life," Willson says. "A lot of bad and a lot of good. But I've never seen anything like this. I know you want what's best for Konnie," he warns Darlene, "but that's not going to be enough. A courthouse can be a very strange and tough place. And it can be very cruel. Like a hospital. It's confusing and scary. If you go on your own, your case could be dismissed or postponed. Time isn't on your side. Abimbola needs to live long enough. The judge will want to be sure that this is what she wants."

Willson understands the cost of failure. "Lots of people want to adopt babies," he says. "Very few are looking for a ten-year-old. As an older child, Konnie would be considered hard to place. She'd likely spend many years being bounced from one foster home to another.

"I can't be your lawyer," Willson explains. "I'm retired. But I can tell you everything you need to know. And on the day, I'm going to pick you up at home and take you to court. I'll be there with you as a friend, holding your hand.

And we're going to walk through this together."

❄ ❄ ❄

That afternoon, Konnie and Willson sit across from each other at their little table in the kitchen on the 6th floor. Konnie stirs her ice cream. She's scared to look up. Willson watches. More than anything, he wants to help her.

"You know something, Konnie?" Willson says. "The hardest job in the world is to be a child growing up. I know that too well. My job was to represent children in court, to protect their rights. I don't do that anymore, but maybe now I can still help you."

Konnie listens to his warm, rumbling voice.

She knows they don't have much time. Four weeks and counting.

She tries to envision the day in court, to imagine the judge with the power to decide her future. Will there be people ready to take her away if the judge says no to Darlene?

THIRTY-SIX

"Please Mama, just a little," Konnie prods. She sits beside her mother and gives her small sips of water, the way one would an injured bird. Sometimes she places a dab of ice cream on a spoon and carefully brings it to her mother's lips.

Abimbola no longer gets out of bed. She hardly speaks, except to worry quietly to her nurses and friends, Colleen and Rita.

Konnie sees the fear on Darlene's face.

A few days later, April 25. The court date is less than two weeks away. When Konnie enters her mother's room, Darlene is already there seated beside the bed, holding her mother's hand. They don't hear her come in.

"Darlene," Abimbola says softly. "I must know that she will be safe. Please, promise me that she will stay with you. Promise me that you will never let her go back to her uncle."

"You need to hold on, Abby," Darlene whispers. "You need to live for this to work."

THIRTY-SEVEN

The night before the court date, Konnie and Darlene sit together at the kitchen table. Darlene rehearses the details out loud, studies the documents one last time.

Beside her, Konnie watches. She watches and draws. A picture of Princess, now fast asleep on her lap. And one of Darlene's mother's dog—a golden retriever named Tyler. With her finger, Konnie smudges the colors, blurs the edges.

In bed that night, Konnie tosses and turns. *If the judge says no, I'll run. I'll run and disappear.*

In the middle of the night, she tiptoes into Darlene's room.

"Darlene?" she whispers. Darlene is awake too, sitting upright in bed, surrounded by the documents. "I can't sleep," Konnie says. "Can I stay here with you tonight?"

Konnie curls up on the opposite side of the bed. If there is any comfort for her this night, it comes from the rhythm of Darlene's breath.

THIRTY-EIGHT

Konnie wakes to the sound of a whistling kettle. Darlene is making tea. Konnie opens her eyes and then shuts them again. Mostly, she wants this day to disappear. To not happen. But a small part of her wants to get it over with. She hates the waiting. The not knowing. She gets dressed and puts on her wishbone necklace and the denim Tinkerbell jacket. Anything to bring good luck today. She pulls out her knapsack and begins to fill it with a few things. Just in case.

At breakfast, she can tell Darlene is nervous. Brow furrowed, forehead creased, cheeks red. Too much smiling. Darlene keeps thinking she's lost something—her keys, her phone, her wallet. She can't keep anything straight this morning. She hardly touches her food.

And then, a loud knock at the door. Konnie jumps and looks through the window.

"Willson!" she calls out. He's here. Just as he promised.

"Wasn't sure you'd let me in!" he winks.

Darlene hardly says a word. She grips the package of documents tightly. Sara and Kayden stand at the door. Sara puts her hands on Konnie's shoulders.

"I know we've had our rough patches, Konnie, but you're one of us now. My little sister."

Konnie likes the sound of it, the taste of it. *A sister*. And Kayden, her own little nephew. And then she feels a stab of fear.

Is it possible to find and lose a family at the very same moment?

THIRTY-NINE

Willson talks in the car all the way to the courthouse.

"The judge will ask questions. All you have to do is tell the truth. Only answer the questions you're asked and keep it short."

It *sounds* simple enough, but Konnie knows there's nothing simple about this. They all know.

Armed security guards stand at the courthouse entrance. There are body scanners, metal detectors. Konnie's heart gallops inside her chest.

The courthouse is busy. People hurry in all directions. Darlene, Konnie, and Willson approach a desk to check in.

"Looks like you're missing some signatures," the clerk says. "Let's reschedule. Give you some time to get this sorted out."

Reschedule?

"No," Willson says firmly. "We're not rescheduling. It's not an option in this case. We'll get those signatures. We're going to get this done today, no matter what."

A few more stern words with the clerk, and they're on their way.

Willson walks briskly through the courthouse. In his hands, the stack of papers.

"James!" Willson calls out to man, a lawyer he recognizes in the hallway.

"Willson. How are you, old friend?"

"Fine, fine, but no time to talk. I need a favor…fast." Willson shows him the documents. James signs on the spot. Willson grabs the paper, raises his hand in thanks, and begins to run. Darlene and Konnie run too. They stop short in front of a closed door.

Courtroom B.

When they enter together, Darlene is still panting. "Willson," she whispers, "courtrooms make me feel like I'm in trouble. What if they want to see Abby? What if the judge says no?"

Konnie checks out the room. There's a clerk and a court reporter. Several rows of long wooden benches. In the center at the front, is the judge's elevated bench. They take their seats.

Konnie sits between Darlene and Willson, holding Darlene's hand. She listens to the lull of Willson's long deep breaths. Slowly, she turns her head and places her other hand on his. She stares straight ahead, repeating Willson's instructions. On her tongue, the bitter taste of fear.

"All rise," the clerk announces. The doors swing open. The judge enters. Konnie can't believe her eyes.

FORTY

Brown hair. Brown skin. All this time, Konnie has pictured the cartoon version of a judge—a tall, older man with a thick, curly white wig and white skin. Instead, the judge is a tiny woman. A tiny brown woman in a long black robe.

Justice Manjusha Pawagi scans the room.

"Willson McTavish!" she says, surprised. "What are *you* doing here?" Justice Pawagi had at one time been a law student in Willson's office, the Office of the Children's Lawyer.

What a lucky coincidence.

"Hello, Your Honor," Willson says respectfully. "I'm here supporting a friend."

Justice Pawagi sits quietly and reads through the documents. When she's done, she looks up and turns to Konnie and asks her to say her full name. Konnie's legs feel like jelly.

"Do you understand why you're here today, Konisola?" the judge asks.

"Yes," she whispers. She can hardly hear her own voice. But Willson's advice comes back to her. *Loud and clear, so the judge can hear you.*

"Darlene wants me to live with her." She stops for a moment, draws in another breath and then says the impossible. "Even after my mom dies."

She can feel the judge watching her closely.

"Is that what you want too?" the judge asks.

"Yes," she says.

"Do you feel comfortable and safe in Darlene's home?"

"Yes. I was scared at first. But not anymore. Now I'm scared you might take me away from her."

Judge Pawagi then turns to Darlene and

asks her a string of questions. About Abimbola's health. About Konnie's life back home. About her future. And, most importantly, she asks, "Is the mother in agreement with your application?"

Darlene's back is dripping with perspiration. She straightens herself and answers.

"I'm not a blood relative, Your Honor, but I love Konisola as if she were my own. I've been caring for her for close to a year now. I'd like to continue to take care of her. Forever. Her mother wants that too. Very much."

In the courtroom, all is quiet. The only sounds are those of the judge turning the pages of the documents. The judge, Willson has told them, will have to think of the facts, of the law, and of Konisola's future. Out of the corner of her eye, Konnie glances at Darlene, eyes closed, lips moving slightly. Konnie knows she's praying. Konnie prays too.

They wait. And wait.

At last, Justice Pawagi looks at Darlene and Konisola. "Darlene Priestman…" she says.

A small sound comes out of Konnie's throat.

"…I hereby award you legal custody of Konisola. It is a privilege to sign this order."

Konnie hears but doesn't quite believe. She looks at Darlene.

Is it true? Did I hear her words correctly?

Yes. Darlene heard them too.

Darlene pulls Konnie in and holds her close. And Konnie wraps her arms tightly around Darlene.

❄ ❄ ❄

Darlene turns to Willson. His eyes are wet. "Thank you," she whispers. "I could never have done this without you."

"Darlene," he says, "we all want this in our lives, don't we? To help people. We're here for a second. Fourteen billion years, and we're here for a second. So, this day worked. I'm just lucky I got to be here, that's all. This feels like the finest day of my life."

❄ ❄ ❄

Konnie and Darlene hurry to the hospital. There's no time to lose.

Konnie sits carefully on the bed. Her mother is groggy, half-asleep from the pain medicine. Konnie has to make sure she hears her clearly. Understands. She leans in close and lifts her mother's hand to her face.

"The judge said yes, Mama. The judge said yes."

FORTY-ONE

That night, Konnie goes back to the hospital.

She unfolds the large, layered piece of fabric. The purple and blue shawl she's worked on for so many weeks.

"Look, Mama. I made this for you," Konnie says, and holds it up for her mother to see. "Do you like it?"

It's the length of Konnie's outstretched arms. Konnie's hands are stamped all over it in ultramarine. And around the edges, in big bold letters, **LOVE MOM. LOVE MOM. LOVE MOM.**

"It is beautiful, Konisola," she whispers. "Like you."

Konnie takes the shawl and drapes it over her mother's body. Then, very carefully, she crawls into bed beside her.

EPILOGUE

On a beautiful and sunny Saturday morning in June, Konnie was horsing around in the backyard. Darlene sat on the stoop, watching her. Inside the house, the phone rang. Darlene ignored it. Then her cell phone rang. It was a nurse from the hospital.

Abimbola had died.

Colleen had watched over her the night before. Tried to keep her comfortable. She covered her with the shawl that Konnie had made. It was almost as if Konnie was with her mother, holding her, until the very end.

Two days later, Konnie's mother was buried. Following Abimbola's wishes, Darlene arranged for a Muslim burial. Konnie was there, holding on tightly to Darlene. Close beside her, Darlene's mother.

Members of the Muslim community—complete strangers—were there too, to pay their respects, to show support. A Muslim cleric, an imam, recited prayers.

Konnie stood holding a purple and blue bundle. She picked up a handful of soil to throw into the hole in the ground, as instructed by the burial society. At the last second, before anyone could stop her, she placed the soil in the shawl she had made and let it fall into the grave.

In the weeks and months that followed Abimbola's death, there were many offers of help. Nurses from the hospital collected furniture for Konnie's bedroom. A teacher at Konnie's school offered to braid her hair the way her mother had. Two of Abimbola's doctors helped to pay for Konnie's dance lessons.

And the hospital gave Darlene time off work to spend with Konnie.

A remarkable set of coincidences and pieces of good luck followed Konnie through her time of darkness, upheaval, and loss. Ayo, Nurse Colleen, Nurse Rita, Dr. Banerji, retired Children's Lawyer Willson, Justice Pawagi, Sara, Kayden, and, of course, Abimbola and Darlene, all formed an invisible circle around Konisola. Each one of them happened to be in just the right place at the very time they were needed. Each did what they could, what they knew they had it in them to do. Without any one of them, Konnie's story might have ended very differently.

Today, Konnie continues to draw and paint. She loves to dance—ballet, tap, hip-hop, and jazz—she plays lacrosse, and swims in the lake at the cottage. She and Darlene now live with Darlene's mother, Betty, along with Princess the cat and Tyler the golden retriever. Sara is married. Kayden is growing. And there's a new little member of the family—a niece for Konnie.

"It's a crazy household," Darlene says. "One big, mixed up family. But it works for us. It works."

As soon as she could, Darlene adopted Konnie, just as she had promised she would. Justice Manjusha Pawagi signed the documents.

Konnie officially changed her name to include her mother's *and* Darlene's. Her full name is now Konisola Abimbola Priestman.

Abimbola left Konnie all that she had.
A memory box made of a dark wood.
Inside, some gold hoop earrings.
A few bracelets. A thick necklace.
A worn, pink leather wallet.
A slim red diary.
A photo of a woman and a young girl.
These are her most precious possessions.

End

*Konnie is now a teenager.
She is pictured here with
her mother, Darlene.*

ACKNOWLEDGMENTS

Thank you, above all, to Konnie and Darlene Priestman for entrusting me with their remarkable story. I am as taken with its poignant beauty today as I was the first time I stumbled upon it. I am profoundly grateful for their openness, honesty, and generosity.

Thank you to Margie Wolfe—the wise, colorful, and gutsy publisher of Second Story Press—who believed this story deserved to be shared with young readers. She took a leap of faith, guided me, spurred me on, and then waited patiently.

To Managing Editor, Kathryn Cole, for

seeing this story through to completion. I benefited greatly from her keen insights, her eagle eye, her gentle hand.

To Melissa Kaita, Emma Rodgers, and the great team at Second Story Press.

To Heather Camlot for important editorial suggestions and thoughtful comments.

To Sara Priestman, Colleen Johnson, Willson McTavish, Anna Banerji, and Manjusha Pawagi for sharing their stories with me.

To Francisco Rico-Martinez who graciously answered important refugee questions.

To Helena Hyams and Aaron Fleishman who read early chapters.

To Sophie and Faye Block—14 and 12 years old—who read the manuscript under a tight deadline. Their incisive thoughts and observations, along with many yellow sticky notes, were so very helpful.

To my extraordinary friends and colleagues at CBC Radio's *The Sunday Edition* —my radio home.

To my fabulous sisters, Ariane and Maura Siegel, and their families.

My mother Mireille and my late father Arthur were born into the turbulence of war-torn Europe. Their stories and those of their parents—stretching from Germany, Poland, Belgium, and Trinidad, and finally to Canada—are mapped inside of me.

I am very grateful to two marvelous women.

Leah Levin, my former roommate and lifelong friend, read the manuscript, made invaluable suggestions, talked with me, thought with me, encouraged me. Always with her signature wit.

My close friend and remarkable radio editor, Karen Levine, worked hand-in-hand with me on my radio documentary, *A Place for Konisola*, which first aired on *The Sunday Edition*. Karen once again shared her brilliant editorial instincts and soulful wisdom as I brought this story to life as a book.

Benjamin Tal made room at our dining room table and in our lives so that I could write this story. In moments of doubt, he buoyed me and told me to keep going.

My sons—Noam and Daniel—have lived and grown with Konisola's story since they were toddlers. They insisted that I "tell the part about the judge again." And so I did. Their insatiable curiosity, big hearts, and deep love of stories, inspire me and guide me always.

ABOUT THE AUTHOR

ALISA SIEGEL makes radio documentaries for the Canadian Broadcasting Corporation. Her work has been recognized with many international awards. Her first radio documentary was a story about her father's escape from Germany to the West Indies on the eve of the Second World War. Over the past 20 years, Alisa has produced stories on subjects as varied as the underground railroad for refugees in Fort Erie, daring women artists in 1920s Montreal, the return of the trumpeter swan, Canadian nurses in World War I, and violence in elementary school classrooms. She lives in Toronto with her family.